Latex Clinic
Hentai Stories Of Latex Pleasure

These stories contain adult content and explore complex relationships that may be considered inappropriate or unethical in real-life settings. It is essential to approach real-life situations with care, respect, and consideration for all parties involved.

Hentai is a subgenre of manga and anime that focuses on explicit or pornographic content. It typically involves sexual or erotic themes and is intended for adult audiences. The term "hentai" literally translates to "perverted" or "abnormal" in Japanese. Hentai often features explicit sexual scenes, nudity, and fetishistic content. While some hentai works may have a storyline or plot, the primary focus is usually on sexual content and gratification. It's important to note that hentai is not considered mainstream or widely accepted in Japanese society and is often produced and consumed within niche communities.

Fictional stories should be treated as entertainment and not as a guide for real-life relationships or behavior.

Written by Jenny Lǐ Harvey

Contents

The Latex Clinic 4

    Chapter 1: Examination and Discipline 4

    Chapter 2: Injection and Surrender 7

    Chapter 3: Sensory Play and Tease 11

    Chapter 4: Electro Stimulation and Control 15

    Chapter 5: Role-Play and Domination 19

    Chapter 6: Aftercare and Connection 24

The Latex Ward 28

    Chapter 1: The Latex Ward 28

    Chapter 2: The New Patient 32

    Chapter 3: The Strict Examination 36

    Chapter 4: The Latex Restraints 39

    Chapter 5: The Discipline Session 43

    Chapter 6: The Aftercare 47

Latex Training Academy 51

    Chapter 1: Enrollment 51

    Chapter 2: Dressing the Part 55

    Chapter 3: Anatomy Lessons 59

    Chapter 4: Psychological Dominance 63

    Chapter 5: The Ward Experience 67

    Chapter 6: Graduation 71

The Latex Asylum 76

    Chapter 1: The Intake Assessment 76

    Chapter 2: Therapy Unleashed 79

Chapter 3: A Latex Restriction 83

Chapter 4: The Electrotherapy Experiment 86

Chapter 5: The Power of Sensory Deprivation 90

Chapter 6: Liberation Through Surrender 94

Latex Emergency Response 100

Chapter 1: The Call of Duty 100

Chapter 2: Tangled Desires 104

Chapter 3: A Healing Touch 107

Chapter 4: Intensive Care 110

Chapter 5: The Late-Night Encounter 114

Chapter 6: Unveiling Desires 117

The Latex Research Facility 120

Chapter 1: The Mysterious Facility 120

Chapter 2: The Provocative Assistant 123

Chapter 3: The Latex Experiment 126

Chapter 4: The Bondage Exploration 130

Chapter 5: The Psychological Fusion 134

Chapter 6: The Unveiling 138

The Latex Clinic

Chapter 1: Examination and Discipline

Dr. Victoria Steel exuded an aura of confidence as she stepped into the examination room of her private latex clinic. Her presence commanded attention, and her captivating eyes sparkled with a mix of curiosity and anticipation. Dressed in a form-fitting latex nurse uniform that clung to every curve, she exuded an air of power and seduction.

John, a tall and handsome man with a hidden desire for submission, stood nervously in the middle of the room. His heart raced in his chest as he watched Dr. Steel approach him with slow, deliberate steps. He had long harbored secret fantasies of exploring his submissive side, and today, he would surrender to the capable hands of this alluring dominatrix nurse.

Dr. Steel's voice was silky smooth as she broke the silence, her words laced with authority. "Please undress, John," she commanded, her tone leaving no room for disobedience. Trembling slightly, he quickly shed his clothes, feeling a mix of vulnerability and excitement coursing through his veins. Now standing before her in nothing but his bare skin, he felt truly exposed.

With a swift movement, Dr. Steel retrieved a fresh pair of latex gloves from a nearby counter, snapping them into place with a tantalizing sound that made John's pulse quicken. The anticipation hung heavy in the air as she approached him, her eyes locked onto his, filled with a mixture of tenderness and dominance.

"Take a deep breath, John," she said, her voice calming and reassuring. "I'm going to examine you thoroughly to ensure you receive the proper care and attention."

John nodded, his mouth suddenly dry, and laid himself down on the examination table. The cold surface sent a shiver down his spine, heightening his senses and reminding him of his vulnerability. Dr. Steel moved gracefully, her latex-clad form a vision of sensuality as she prepared the various medical instruments around them.

She began the examination, her gloved hands gliding across John's skin with a delicate touch. The latex gloves provided an extra layer of intimacy, amplifying every sensation as they traced the contours of his body. The doctor's skilled fingers explored his muscles, probed his joints, and checked his vital signs, each touch eliciting a mixture of pleasure and a tinge of pain.

As Dr. Steel worked her way through the examination, she maintained a level of professionalism that mingled effortlessly with her dominant nature. Her voice, commanding and firm, guided John through the process, ensuring his compliance and submission. With each instruction, he found himself surrendering further, losing himself in the blend of vulnerability and trust that enveloped them.

The intensity of the examination heightened as Dr. Steel's gloved hands ventured into more intimate regions. John's breath hitched as she explored his most sensitive areas, pushing the boundaries of his comfort. The dichotomy of pain and pleasure danced in the air, creating a heady cocktail that left him craving more.

Dr. Steel's eyes never wavered, capturing John's gaze with an unwavering intensity. She could sense his desires, his unspoken fantasies, and she expertly played upon them, pushing him to his limits and beyond. She knew exactly how to administer just the right amount of discipline to keep him on the edge, his surrender deepening with every touch.

Throughout the examination, Dr. Steel maintained a delicate balance between nurturing care and strict discipline. She was a master of her craft, knowing precisely how to elicit the desired response from her submissive patients. Her touch was both firm and gentle, her commands both authoritative and soothing.

As the examination neared its conclusion, Dr. Steel leaned over John, her face inches from his, her breath warm against his skin. "You've done well, John," she whispered, her voice a sultry caress. "Your submission is a beautiful thing."

A surge of pride and satisfaction washed over John, mingling with a profound sense of surrender. In that moment, he realized he had embarked on a journey of self-discovery, guided by the capable hands and dominant presence of Dr. Victoria Steel.

The examination ended, but the story of their exploration was just beginning.

Chapter 2: Injection and Surrender

Dr. Victoria Steel led John to a small, sterile room tucked away in the depths of her latex clinic. The walls were pristine white, adorned with shelves upon shelves of neatly organized medical supplies. A single examination chair stood in the center, its cold metal frame accentuated by black leather restraints.

John's heart raced in his chest as he gazed around the room, a mixture of anticipation and trepidation building within him. He knew that this injection would be more than just a routine medical procedure. It would be an act of surrender, a symbol of his trust in Dr. Steel's capable hands.

"Please, have a seat," Dr. Steel's voice resonated, breaking through his thoughts. Her tone was both commanding and reassuring, her gaze penetrating deep into his soul. She exuded confidence and power, her latex-clad figure a mesmerizing sight.

John obeyed, his limbs feeling heavy with anticipation as he lowered himself onto the examination chair. The cool leather pressed against his bare skin, sending a shiver of excitement down his spine. He watched with bated breath as Dr. Steel moved gracefully around the room, her gloved hands expertly preparing the necessary supplies.

Her latex gloves glistened under the bright lights, a stark contrast against her porcelain skin. John couldn't help but feel a surge of desire at the sight, his body responding to the inherent sensuality of the moment. He was captivated by her every move, the way she handled the syringe with such precision and control.

Dr. Steel approached him, the scent of latex filling the air, mingling with the intoxicating aroma of arousal. She positioned herself at his side, her proximity sending a surge of electricity through his veins. Their eyes locked, and time seemed to stand still as she raised the syringe, its silver glint reflecting the uncertainty and longing in John's eyes.

"Relax, John," Dr. Steel whispered, her voice a soothing balm against his restless soul. "Trust me, and let go."

He nodded, surrendering himself to her with a mix of anticipation and vulnerability. As her gloved fingers traced the outline of his arm, a tingling sensation coursed through his body. The latex felt smooth against his skin, creating an intimate connection between them.

With a steady hand, Dr. Steel positioned the needle against his flesh, its cold touch sending a jolt of anticipation through his veins. She applied gentle pressure, and he felt the sharp prick as the needle penetrated his skin. A gasp escaped his lips, a mingling of pain and pleasure.

But it was more than just a physical sensation. As the plunger was depressed, a rush of endorphins flooded his system, blending with the sense of submission and trust that he had willingly placed in Dr. Steel's hands. It was a potent cocktail that ignited a fire within him, a fire fueled by the intoxicating mix of latex and desire.

Dr. Steel watched his reaction intently, her eyes alight with a primal hunger. She understood the power she held, not just as a medical professional but as a dominant force in this unique world they had created. Her gaze was a potent combination of compassion and dominance, a magnetic pull that drew John further into the depths of his desires.

As the injection reached its completion, Dr. Steel withdrew the needle, her touch lingering for a moment longer than necessary. She pressed a gloved finger against the puncture site, applying gentle pressure to ensure there was no bleeding.

John's eyes never wavered from her, his gaze locked onto hers as she leaned closer. The scent of latex engulfed him, and he felt a surge of heat radiating between them. He longed for her touch, for the reassurance that she alone could provide.

But Dr. Steel, ever the master of control, pulled away, a small smile playing at the corners of her lips. "You did well, John," she murmured, her voice a low purr that sent shivers down his spine. "But our journey has only just begun."

With those words, she turned and moved toward the door, leaving him there, breathless and yearning for more. The injection had marked the first step in their exploration, a tantalizing taste of the power dynamics that lay ahead.

John remained in the examination chair, his body humming with a potent mix of pleasure and submission. He knew that he had surrendered to a force greater than himself, one that would guide him through a labyrinth of desire and pleasure. Dr. Victoria Steel had become the conductor of his deepest fantasies, and he was ready to follow her lead into the intoxicating world of latex and surrender.

Chapter 3: Sensory Play and Tease

In the dimly lit room of the latex clinic, Dr. Victoria Steel led John to the threshold of sensory exploration and exquisite tease. The air was thick with anticipation as they stepped into a chamber adorned with an array of intriguing instruments, each promising an intoxicating mixture of pleasure and submission.

John's heart raced as he gazed at the room's enigmatic ambiance. Shadows danced across the walls, and a faint scent of latex lingered, heightening his senses. The walls were adorned with mirrors strategically placed to reflect every tantalizing moment, ensuring that he never missed a single captivating detail.

Dr. Steel, a vision of power and beauty in her skintight latex nurse uniform, moved with grace and confidence. Her commanding presence wrapped around John like a seductive embrace, igniting a hunger within him that he had never known before.

With a glance that pierced his soul, Dr. Steel guided John toward a padded table at the center of the room. Its surface was plush and inviting, beckoning him to surrender his body to the sensations that awaited him. He felt a tingle of excitement and a slight tremor of apprehension, knowing that he was about to embark on an unforgettable journey of pleasure and surrender.

As John laid himself down on the table, the cool touch of the latex against his skin sent shivers of delight down his spine. His body, clad in a form-fitting latex suit that mirrored Dr. Steel's attire, became a canvas for the intricate play of sensation and submission that was about to unfold.

Dr. Steel, her voice a symphony of both command and tenderness, began to explore his body with her gloved hands. Each caress, each stroke, ignited a fire within him, awakening nerve endings that had long lain dormant. Her touch was simultaneously gentle and demanding, expertly guiding him deeper into a state of vulnerability and bliss.

Moving with practiced precision, Dr. Steel revealed an assortment of instruments designed to tease and tantalize the senses. A feathered tickler danced across John's flesh, tracing delicate patterns that sent waves of pleasure radiating through his entire being. The soft bristles of a brush caressed his skin, setting it ablaze with a tingling warmth that made him arch his back in sheer ecstasy.

But it was the introduction of a small, vibrating device that truly pushed John to the brink of sensory overload. As Dr. Steel pressed the device against his most sensitive areas, the hum of pleasure reverberated through his body, unraveling his control thread by thread. He was a captive to the sensations, his mind consumed by a cocktail of desire, surrender, and an insatiable craving for more.

With each passing moment, Dr. Steel skillfully escalated the intensity, pushing him to new heights of pleasure and surrender. Her mastery over his senses was awe-inspiring, her understanding of his desires a testament to her expertise as a dominatrix nurse. She knew exactly how far to push him, how to balance moments of exquisite tease with bursts of overwhelming sensation.

And as John teetered on the edge of his limits, Dr. Steel would deftly reign him in, bringing him back from the precipice, only to propel him forward once again. The dance of pleasure and surrender became a symphony, conducted by her latex-clad hands, each note echoing through his veins, resonating with the deepest corners of his soul.

Time seemed to lose all meaning in that room of sensory exploration. Every touch, every whisper, every sound was amplified, magnified to create a world where there was only John, Dr. Steel, and the intoxicating realm of pleasure they had crafted together. And in that heightened state, he found liberation in his submission, a surrender that unlocked a raw, primal connection between them.

As the session drew to a close, Dr. Steel's touch gentled, her hands soothing the heightened sensitivity of his skin. She tenderly caressed him, grounding him after the intense journey they had embarked upon. Their eyes met, and in that shared gaze, John saw a reflection of his own desires, mirrored in the depths of her unwavering gaze.

The room seemed to hold its breath as they lingered in that moment of connection, suspended in time. The journey of sensory exploration had come to an end, but its impact would forever be etched into their memories. The seductive world of latex, dominance, and submission had enveloped them, leaving them forever changed, their souls forever entwined in the delicious embrace of pleasure and surrender.

With a final, lingering touch, Dr. Steel guided John back to himself, back to the realm outside the latex clinic. But the echoes of their encounter would continue to reverberate, a melody that would play on, resonating within them, a constant reminder of the depths of desire and the power of surrender that they had discovered together.

Chapter 4: Electro Stimulation and Control

Dr. Victoria Steel led John through the labyrinthine corridors of her private latex clinic until they reached a secluded room, bathed in an ethereal glow of subdued lighting. The room hummed with anticipation, and a hint of nervous excitement wafted in the air. John's eyes darted around, taking in the various electrical devices and restraints that adorned the room. It was as if he had entered an otherworldly realm, where pleasure and pain danced in perfect harmony.

His heart thumped in his chest as Dr. Steel closed the door behind them, her eyes glinting with a mixture of authority and sensuality. She exuded an overwhelming aura of dominance, her latex-clad figure accentuating her curves and emphasizing her power. It was a sight that both thrilled and intimidated John, igniting a fire deep within him.

"Undress," Dr. Steel commanded, her voice laced with firmness. John complied, slowly peeling off his clothes, feeling the cool air brush against his exposed skin. He stood there, vulnerable and naked, while Dr. Steel observed him with an intensity that sent shivers down his spine.

With measured steps, Dr. Steel approached him, her latex-gloved hand tracing a teasing path along his chest. She circled him like a predator, her eyes devouring every inch of his body, stoking the flames of his desire. The anticipation mounted, leaving John on the precipice of ecstasy and surrender.

Reaching a table adorned with an array of metallic implements, Dr. Steel gestured for John to lie down. The table was covered in a sleek, black latex sheet, its glossy surface reflecting the glimmer of the room's dim lights. As John settled onto the table, his body taut with anticipation, Dr. Steel began securing him in place, using latex restraints that encased his wrists and ankles.

The room buzzed with a palpable tension as Dr. Steel prepared the electrical devices. John's eyes widened as he watched her deftly attach electrodes to various strategic points on his body. The metallic tendrils clung to his skin, forming a delicate web of connection. He couldn't help but tremble in both fear and arousal at the thought of the pulsating current that awaited him.

Dr. Steel moved closer, her breath warm against John's ear. "You are mine now," she whispered, her voice dripping with authority and seduction. "You will surrender to my control, my dear John."

As if on cue, she flicked a switch, and a surge of electricity coursed through the electrodes, sending a jolt of sensation straight to John's core. His body arched, a gasp escaping his lips as pleasure and pain collided, melding into a symphony of ecstasy. Dr. Steel, an orchestrator of desire, adjusted the intensity, modulating the current to both tease and push John's limits.

With each surge of electricity, John's world narrowed down to the electrifying sensations that coursed through his body. His mind transcended the realm of everyday existence, soaring into a heightened state of bliss. Dr. Steel, a master of control, guided him through the waves of pleasure, alternating between moments of exquisite torment and overwhelming release.

Time ceased to exist as John's senses became entangled in a dance of surrender. The electricity, once a foreign entity, had woven itself into the fabric of his being, electrifying his desires and awakening a dormant hunger within him. Dr. Steel, a conduit of power, reveled in the control she wielded, exploring the intricate balance between pain and pleasure.

As the session neared its crescendo, Dr. Steel gradually decreased the intensity of the electrical current, allowing John to descend from the heights of euphoria. His body lay spent, covered in a sheen of sweat, his mind floating in a haze of satisfaction and bliss.

Dr. Steel, her eyes gleaming with a mix of satisfaction and tenderness, released John from his restraints. She helped him sit up, his limbs feeling both heavy and light, as if he had been transported to a different realm and brought back to reality all at once.

They sat together on the edge of the table, their breaths mingling in the air. Dr. Steel's hand gently cradled John's face, her touch a balm that soothed his electrified senses. In that moment, he felt a profound connection, a shared understanding of the depths they had explored together.

"You were magnificent," Dr. Steel murmured, her voice a delicate caress. "You trusted me, and I guided you through an experience that few are brave enough to seek."

John looked into her eyes, his heart brimming with gratitude and awe. "Thank you, Dr. Steel," he whispered, his voice laced with reverence. "You've shown me a world beyond my wildest dreams."

In that intimate moment, John and Dr. Steel shared a bond forged in the fires of desire and surrender. The latex clinic had become their sanctuary, a place where boundaries blurred and pleasure reigned supreme. As they sat there, basking in the afterglow of their electrifying encounter, they knew that their journey was far from over. Together, they would continue to explore the depths of their desires, in a dance of dominance and submission that would forever bind them.

Chapter 5: Role-Play and Domination

Dr. Victoria Steel, her eyes ablaze with a smoldering dominance, led John into a room that seemed to pulsate with an undercurrent of forbidden desire. The medical role-play chamber was unlike anything he had ever seen before. It was a realm where boundaries were blurred, where the lines between pleasure and pain merged in an intoxicating dance.

John's heart raced as he observed the room's meticulously arranged equipment: an imposing medical examination table adorned with restraints, shelves filled with a dizzying array of tantalizing instruments, and a cabinet stocked with an assortment of wickedly delightful surprises. The atmosphere crackled with anticipation, and he felt a heady mix of excitement and trepidation.

Dr. Steel's latex-clad figure seemed to come alive, accentuating every curve of her body. The glossy material clung to her like a second skin, highlighting her authority and sensuality in equal measure. Her commanding presence made it clear that she was the orchestrator of this exquisite play, and John was her willing instrument.

With a flick of her finger, she motioned for him to undress. Every garment that fell to the floor intensified his vulnerability, leaving him exposed not only physically but also emotionally. The air crackled with electricity as he stood before her, completely bare and at her mercy.

"Are you ready to submit?" Dr. Steel's voice, laced with a potent blend of seduction and authority, reverberated through the room, sending shivers down John's spine.

"Yes," he replied, his voice laced with a mix of anticipation and longing.

Dr. Steel circled around him, her eyes taking in every inch of his exposed flesh. Her fingers grazed his skin, leaving a trail of heat in their wake. She leaned in, her breath teasingly close to his ear.

"Today, you are mine," she whispered, her voice a sultry melody that ignited a fire within him. "I will push your limits, taking you to new heights of pleasure and surrender."

A surge of desire coursed through John's veins as he absorbed her words. The anticipation was almost unbearable, but he knew that Dr. Steel's expert guidance would lead him to places he had only dared to dream of.

With a swift motion, she instructed him to lie on the examination table. The coolness of the leather against his skin sent a shiver of anticipation through his body. He willingly surrendered himself to her, his body at her mercy, his mind open to the possibilities that awaited him.

Dr. Steel approached him, her latex-clad body radiating power and control. She began by securing his wrists and ankles with soft, yet unyielding restraints, ensuring that he was completely at her mercy. The feeling of vulnerability mingled with a sense of liberation, as he let go of all control and surrendered himself to her skilled hands.

Her touch was electrifying, alternating between gentle caresses and stinging slaps that sent shockwaves of pleasure coursing through his body. Every sensation was heightened, every touch magnified by the power dynamic between them. His body arched and writhed beneath her, craving more, craving the intoxicating mix of pain and pleasure that only she could provide.

Dr. Steel, in her role as the dominant nurse, continued to push his boundaries. She introduced him to a variety of implements, each one delivering a unique sensation that made him moan with pleasure and ache with desire. The sting of a riding crop, the relentless throb of a flogger, and the rhythmic pulsations of a violet wand—all contributed to an exquisite symphony of sensations that left him breathless and yearning for more.

As the session progressed, Dr. Steel explored the depths of his desires, skillfully weaving a tapestry of dominance and submission that entwined their souls. She unleashed her commanding presence, her voice resonating with authority and desire as she pushed him to his limits.

"Submit," she commanded, her voice laced with a potent mix of dominance and affection. "Embrace the pleasure that comes with surrender. Trust me to guide you, to take you to the edge and bring you back."

And John did. He surrendered himself fully, letting go of all inhibitions, allowing the currents of pleasure and pain to carry him away. The world outside faded into insignificance as his focus narrowed solely on the intoxicating dance between himself and Dr. Steel.

Time seemed to stretch and contract, blurring the boundaries between moments of exquisite agony and euphoric release. Each strike of the implement, each command uttered by Dr. Steel, sent him spiraling deeper into a realm of submission where his every need and desire were met with unwavering attentiveness.

Dr. Steel's dominance was not merely about inflicting pain. It was a delicate dance, a choreography of sensations that awakened dormant desires within him. She knew exactly when to push him to the brink, to grant him release, and when to hold him back, denying him that release until he was begging for it.

Within the confines of the latex-clad room, they surrendered to a dance that transcended the physical. It was an exploration of power and trust, a journey of self-discovery that pushed their boundaries and united their souls in a way that defied conventional understanding.

As the session drew to a close, Dr. Steel released John from his restraints. His body, marked with the remnants of their passionate encounter, tingled with the aftermath of their shared journey. Dr. Steel enveloped him in a tender embrace, her latex-clad body molding against his naked flesh.

"You were magnificent," she whispered, her voice filled with admiration and tenderness. "You trusted me, and I took you to places you've never been before."

John smiled, his heart overflowing with gratitude and a profound sense of connection. In the aftermath of their exploration, he realized that their encounter went far beyond the realm of physical pleasure—it had awakened a deeper understanding of his desires and unveiled a profound connection between them.

In the hallowed sanctuary of the latex clinic, Dr. Victoria Steel and John had ventured into uncharted territory, forging a bond that surpassed the boundaries of their roles. They were united by a shared journey of dominance and submission, forever changed by the intensity of their encounter, and ready to explore the uncharted realms of their desires together.

Chapter 6: Aftercare and Connection

Dr. Victoria Steel led John to the aftercare room, a sanctuary of soft lighting and soothing ambiance. The air was filled with a delicate blend of warmth and tenderness, a stark contrast to the intensity of their previous encounters. Here, in this intimate space, they would explore the deeper connection that lay beneath the latex-clad surface.

Gently guiding John to a plush armchair, Dr. Steel offered him a seat. She moved gracefully, her latex-clad body shimmering under the soft glow of the room. As she sat down beside him, the room seemed to hold its breath, as if anticipating the emotions that would soon unfold.

Their eyes met, a silent understanding passing between them. Dr. Steel's voice, usually commanding and assertive, took on a softer tone. "John, you've shown incredible strength and vulnerability today. I'm here to support you, to offer care beyond the boundaries of our dominant-submissive dynamic."

John's heart fluttered, his breath catching in his chest. He had explored realms of pleasure and submission he never thought possible, but now, in this moment, he longed for something deeper—a connection that transcended their roles.

Dr. Steel leaned in closer, her latex-clad hand reaching out to gently brush against his cheek. The cool, smooth texture of the material sent a shiver down his spine. "Aftercare is just as important as the play itself, John. It's a time to decompress, to process the emotions that arise from our shared experiences."

He nodded, his gaze locked with hers. His mind raced, wondering what lay ahead in this uncharted territory. Dr. Steel's touch was both comforting and arousing, a delicate dance between care and desire.

Dr. Steel reached behind her, her latex-covered fingers grasping a small vial. She held it up, the liquid inside glistening under the soft glow of the room. "This is a special blend of oils, John. It's designed to soothe and nourish your skin, to help you find a sense of peace and tranquility after the intensity of our session."

Intrigued, John watched as Dr. Steel uncapped the vial and poured a few drops onto her gloved palm. The aroma of lavender filled the air, its calming scent permeating the room. With deliberate yet gentle movements, she began to massage the oil into his skin, her touch firm and yet incredibly tender.

The sensation was exquisite. As her hands glided over his body, his muscles relaxed, the tension melting away. Every stroke, every caress seemed to ignite a spark within him, awakening a profound yearning for both physical and emotional connection.

Dr. Steel leaned closer, her lips hovering just inches from his ear. "John, during our time together, I've witnessed your willingness to surrender, to trust me with your deepest desires. You've allowed me to explore the depths of your submission, and for that, I'm grateful."

Her words stirred something within him. He realized that their journey had been about more than just physical pleasure—it was about vulnerability, trust, and the profound connection that blossomed when two souls met in the space between dominance and submission.

Dr. Steel continued her massage, her gloved hands leaving trails of warmth and comfort in their wake. "Aftercare is also about communication, John. It's a time for us to share our thoughts, our feelings. How are you feeling right now?"

John took a deep breath, the scent of lavender filling his lungs. He closed his eyes, searching for the words to convey the depth of his emotions. "Dr. Steel, this experience has been transformative for me. The blend of dominance and care, the power exchange, it's awakened something within me that I never knew existed. I feel both vulnerable and empowered at the same time."

Dr. Steel's touch paused for a moment, her eyes meeting his with an intensity that made his heart race. "John, it's beautiful to witness the awakening of your desires, your exploration of the depths of your being. Know that you're not alone on this journey. I'm here to guide you, to support you as you discover the intricacies of your submission."

Her words washed over him, a soothing balm to his soul. The vulnerability he had shown, the trust he had placed in her hands—it was reciprocated in her commitment to his growth and well-being.

As Dr. Steel continued the massage, their conversation deepened, exploring the nuances of their experiences, their desires, and their hopes for the future. Time seemed to stand still as they delved into the depths of their connection, baring their souls to one another.

Eventually, the massage came to an end, but the connection they had forged remained. Dr. Steel gazed into John's eyes, a soft smile playing on her lips. "John, this journey we've embarked upon is not confined to the walls of the latex clinic. It's an exploration of self, of trust, and of the beauty that lies within the surrender to our desires."

He nodded, his heart swelling with gratitude for the extraordinary woman before him. In her latex-clad presence, he had discovered a safe space to explore his most secret desires, his truest self.

Dr. Steel rose from her seat, her latex-clad form radiant under the gentle light. She extended a gloved hand towards him, an invitation to stand alongside her. "John, let's embrace this connection, this journey, together. Beyond the confines of our sessions, let us explore the infinite possibilities that lie ahead."

John took her hand, his heart full of anticipation for the future that awaited them. As they walked out of the aftercare room, the world seemed brighter, filled with endless potential and the beauty of surrender. In the embrace of their shared desires, they would continue to explore the depths of their connection, bound by latex and love, forever entwined in the dance of dominance and submission.

The Latex Ward

Chapter 1: The Latex Ward

Nurse Cassandra's heart raced as she entered the dimly lit Latex Ward, her short red hair falling in playful curls around her face. The soft glow of the overhead lights cast an otherworldly ambiance on the room, emphasizing the sterile whiteness of the walls and the pristine latex covering every surface. The scent of rubber, mixed with a subtle hint of arousal, filled her senses, awakening a familiar longing within her.

Her latex uniform clung to her like a second skin, molding to her every curve with a tantalizing tightness. The form-fitting garment accentuated her petite yet shapely figure, the glossy material reflecting the light and amplifying her allure. The high collar encircled her delicate neck, hinting at a sense of control and authority, while the plunging neckline teased a tantalizing glimpse of her cleavage, leaving the observer wanting more.

With each click of her stiletto heels on the polished floor, Nurse Cassandra exuded a captivating mix of confidence and sensuality. Her presence commanded attention, drawing the gazes of both patients and staff alike. She relished the power she held over those within the Latex Ward, the allure of her latex-clad persona granting her the ability to guide willing souls through a journey of pleasure and surrender.

As she strode past the rows of hospital beds, her sharp emerald eyes scanned the room, taking in the scene before her. Patients, dressed in their own latex attire, occupied the beds, some with eyes filled with anticipation, others displaying a mixture of excitement and nervousness. The air was heavy with an unspoken understanding, a shared desire for exploration and fulfillment.

Nurse Cassandra's gaze settled on a young man in his late twenties, lying in Bed 305. His hazel eyes widened as he caught sight of her approaching, and a faint blush tinted his cheeks. She could sense his curiosity and longing, the desire to relinquish control and surrender to her latex-clad dominance.

With a subtle gesture, Nurse Cassandra beckoned the young man to follow her. He obeyed, his footsteps hesitant at first but growing bolder with each stride. She led him to a small private examination room, the sound of their footsteps echoing off the sterile walls, adding an intimate rhythm to their encounter.

Inside the room, the lighting was softer, casting a warm, inviting glow. The atmosphere shifted, transitioning from the clinical sterility of the ward to a more intimate setting. The room was adorned with various medical instruments, each meticulously cleaned and laid out with precision. The walls were adorned with mirrors, strategically placed to capture and reflect every moment of their encounter.

Nurse Cassandra turned to face her patient, her gaze piercing through him with a mix of compassion and authority. "Undress," she commanded, her voice silky smooth, laced with a hint of anticipation. Her eyes never left his as he fumbled to remove his clothing, his hands trembling with a combination of excitement and nervousness.

As the young man stood before her, completely exposed, Nurse Cassandra drank in the sight before her. She appreciated the vulnerability and trust he placed in her hands. His toned physique displayed a combination of strength and vulnerability, a canvas ready to be explored and pleasured.

With measured steps, she circled him, her fingertips grazing the edges of his skin, leaving a trail of goosebumps in their wake. The latex of her gloves whispered against his flesh, a gentle caress that ignited his senses. She watched as his muscles tensed and relaxed under her touch, a dance of control and submission unfolding before her eyes.

"Your body is mine to explore, to awaken," Nurse Cassandra murmured, her voice a seductive whisper. "Every inch of your skin is mine to possess, to pleasure, and to dominate."

With that declaration, Nurse Cassandra's touch became bolder, more demanding. Her gloved hand glided over his chest, tracing the lines of his defined muscles, leaving no inch of him untouched. She relished the way his breath hitched and his body quivered, the delicious mix of vulnerability and excitement fueling her own desires.

As her hand descended lower, grazing his abdomen, the young man's breathing quickened, his anticipation palpable. Nurse Cassandra's fingers dipped lower still, exploring the territory that lay hidden beneath the fabric of his desire. Her touch was deliberate, expertly navigating the contours of his manhood, teasing and toying with his pleasure.

She sensed his need, his desperation for release, but she denied him that satisfaction. Her touch withdrew, leaving him hanging on the precipice of pleasure, his eyes begging for more. "Patience," she whispered, her voice dripping with desire and authority. "Patience, my dear. The best is yet to come."

Nurse Cassandra stepped away, her gaze fixed upon her patient's desire-stricken face. The air between them crackled with unspoken promises and untamed passion. In that moment, they both understood that their journey had only just begun, and within the confines of the Latex Ward, their desires would be indulged, their boundaries tested, and their pleasure explored to its fullest extent.

With a mischievous smile playing upon her lips, Nurse Cassandra extended her hand, her latex-clad fingers inviting him to take the next step. And in that delicate moment, the young man willingly surrendered himself to the latex-clad nurse, knowing that within her skilled hands, he would find the fulfillment he sought.

Chapter 2: The New Patient

Nurse Cassandra, a stunning 23-year-old with short fiery red hair, stood outside Room 203, her heart pounding with anticipation. She adjusted the tightness of her latex uniform, ensuring every curve was accentuated to perfection. The room beyond held a new patient, Mark, a man who sought the unconventional treatments that only the Latex Ward could provide.

Taking a deep breath, Nurse Cassandra pushed open the door, her presence commanding and dominant. Mark, a handsome man in his early thirties, looked up from his hospital bed, his eyes widening at the sight of the alluring nurse.

"Good evening, Mark," Nurse Cassandra purred, her voice laced with a hint of authority. "I'm Nurse Cassandra, and I'll be taking care of you tonight."

Mark swallowed hard, his gaze locked on her latex-clad form. He had heard whispers about the Latex Ward, about the unorthodox methods employed by the nurses. His curiosity had driven him to this moment, to submit himself to the hands of Nurse Cassandra and her unique brand of care.

"Nurse Cassandra," Mark stammered, his voice betraying his nervousness. "I... I've heard things. I want to experience something different, something extraordinary."

A knowing smile tugged at the corners of Nurse Cassandra's lips as she approached the bedside, her heels clicking with each step. She reached out and gently ran a latex-gloved finger along the side of Mark's face, the coolness of the rubber sending shivers down his spine.

"You're in the right place, Mark," she murmured, her voice dripping with confidence. "In this ward, we offer treatments that explore the boundaries between pleasure and pain, power and submission. Are you ready to surrender yourself to my care?"

Mark hesitated for a moment, his eyes locked with Nurse Cassandra's intense gaze. He could sense the power she held, the control she exuded. In that moment, he knew he was ready to surrender, to experience something beyond the realm of ordinary.

"Yes, Nurse Cassandra," Mark whispered, his voice barely audible. "I'm ready."

Nurse Cassandra's smile widened as she motioned for Mark to rise from the bed. She led him to a small corner of the room, where a sleek black leather chair awaited. With a soft gesture, she urged Mark to sit, his anticipation building with every passing second.

Slowly, Nurse Cassandra circled the chair, her latex-clad body brushing against Mark's exposed arm, sending jolts of electricity through his veins. She leaned in, her warm breath caressing his ear, her voice barely above a whisper.

"Mark, close your eyes," she commanded softly. "Let yourself sink into the darkness, and trust that I will guide you through an extraordinary journey."

Mark complied, his eyelids fluttering shut, a sense of vulnerability washing over him. He felt Nurse Cassandra's presence behind him, her fingertips trailing along his bare shoulders, leaving a trail of fire in their wake.

The room fell into a hushed silence, broken only by the sound of Nurse Cassandra's latex-clad movements. Her hands glided down Mark's back, tracing the contours of his body, awakening every nerve. A shiver coursed through him as she leaned in, her lips hovering just above his ear.

"Mark, I want you to imagine a world where the boundaries of pleasure and pain blur," she whispered, her voice husky with desire. "A world where the touch of latex against your skin becomes intoxicating, a world where your desires are explored and embraced."

As Nurse Cassandra spoke, she retrieved a pair of latex gloves from a nearby tray. The sound of the latex stretching and snapping into place filled the room, heightening Mark's senses. He could feel the anticipation building, his body humming with a mix of nerves and excitement.

With deliberate slowness, Nurse Cassandra brought her hands to Mark's shoulders, her gloved fingertips gliding across his skin. The sensation was electrifying, each touch sending waves of pleasure through his body. Her hands trailed lower, expertly massaging his back, her movements alternating between firm pressure and feather-light caresses.

"Relax, Mark," she cooed, her voice a gentle lullaby. "Let go of any inhibitions, surrender yourself to the sensations coursing through you. Trust me to guide you through this experience."

Mark obeyed, allowing the sensations to wash over him, surrendering to the trust he had placed in Nurse Cassandra. The latex-clad nurse continued her ministrations, her hands exploring every inch of his exposed flesh, her touch a delicate dance between ecstasy and torment.

As the minutes turned into an eternity, Nurse Cassandra's movements shifted, her hands gliding down Mark's back and reaching the edge of his waistband. A low moan escaped his lips as she leaned in, her lips grazing his earlobe.

"Mark, you're doing so well," she murmured, her voice filled with a mix of admiration and arousal. "But the journey has only just begun. Are you ready for what lies ahead?"

Mark's heart raced, his body aflame with desire. He nodded, his lips parting in a silent plea for more. He was ready to surrender himself completely, to experience the extraordinary world that Nurse Cassandra promised.

With a wicked smile, Nurse Cassandra withdrew her hands, leaving Mark yearning for her touch. The momentary absence left a void, an ache that only she could fill. And as Nurse Cassandra continued to guide him through the depths of the Latex Ward, Mark knew that he had entered a realm where pleasure and pain intertwined, where the latex-clad nurse held the key to his ultimate liberation.

Chapter 3: The Strict Examination

Nurse Cassandra watched as Mark undressed, her gaze filled with a potent mix of authority and desire. His eyes were fixated on her, his breaths shallow and expectant. As he stood before her, naked and vulnerable, she couldn't help but appreciate the sight before her—the defined contours of his muscular physique, the way his skin glistened with a thin sheen of anticipation.

With a flick of her wrist, Nurse Cassandra motioned for Mark to step onto the examination table, its surface adorned with a latex cover that clung to every curve. She reached for a pair of latex gloves, the material stretching effortlessly over her slender fingers. The slight rasp of latex against latex filled the room as she snapped them into place, her eyes never leaving Mark's form.

"Please lie down," Nurse Cassandra instructed, her voice a seductive purr, a blend of command and allure. Mark complied, his body sinking into the cool surface of the table. The room was hushed, tension thickening the air, as Nurse Cassandra moved around him, her every step deliberate and measured.

Her fingers glided across his bare chest, tracing a path over his taut abdomen, before descending lower, to where desire pulsed with every heartbeat. She pressed her palm against his skin, feeling the rapid rise and fall of his chest, the hitch in his breath. Mark's body arched subtly under her touch, a silent plea for more.

Nurse Cassandra retrieved a stethoscope from the nearby tray, its shiny black tubing matching the latex ensemble that adorned her body. She leaned in close, the scent of rubber mingling with the warmth of their bodies. As she positioned the cold metal disc against his chest, a shudder coursed through Mark's frame, his eyes fluttering closed.

The nurse listened intently, her ear pressed to the stethoscope, her focus solely on the rhythmic cadence of his heart. But her touch, her proximity, spoke of something deeper—a connection that extended beyond the realms of conventional medicine. She reveled in the power she held over him, the ability to elicit such primal responses with her mere presence.

Moving with deliberate precision, Nurse Cassandra moved the stethoscope lower, capturing the symphony of his heartbeat as it pulsed beneath his ribcage. The sounds filled her ears, a rhythmic melody that mirrored the awakening desires within them both. She shifted her gaze upward, locking eyes with Mark, their silent agreement forged in a mutual understanding of the forbidden.

Sensing his unspoken need, Nurse Cassandra allowed her fingers to wander, tracing invisible patterns along his inner thighs. She delighted in the sharp intake of his breath, the way his muscles tensed beneath her touch. Slowly, her fingers crept higher, teasing the boundaries of pleasure, until she found the source of his most intimate yearnings.

Mark's eyes widened, his lips parting in a silent gasp as Nurse Cassandra's fingers grazed the sensitive skin. A surge of electricity coursed through him, igniting a fire that consumed his senses. The lines between professional and personal blurred, and he surrendered himself entirely to the exquisite torment of her touch.

Nurse Cassandra leaned in closer, her breath warm against his ear, her voice laced with a subtle dominance that sent shivers down his spine. "Relax, Mark," she whispered, her words like a command. "You're in good hands."

And as her fingers worked their magic, tracing circles of pleasure, Mark's body succumbed to a symphony of sensations. Every nerve ending awakened, every touch amplified, until he was teetering on the precipice of ecstasy. Nurse Cassandra held him there, her touch a masterful dance of control and release, until the dam finally broke, and waves of pleasure crashed over him in glorious surrender.

As the echoes of their shared intimacy reverberated through the room, Nurse Cassandra retreated with a satisfied smile, her eyes alight with a knowing gleam. She had witnessed the depths of his desires, tasted the power that surged between them, and she knew their journey had only just begun.

Mark was left breathless and craving more, aching for the next encounter in the Latex Ward, where Nurse Cassandra's dominance and his submission would intertwine once again.

Chapter 4: The Latex Restraints

Nurse Cassandra's emerald eyes glinted mischievously as she watched Mark, her newest submissive patient, lie on the examination table. The room was bathed in a soft, ambient glow, casting shadows that danced across the walls. Her short red hair framed her delicate face, accentuating her youthful allure and dominant presence.

With a slow, deliberate movement, Nurse Cassandra approached Mark, her latex-clad body caressing the air. The tight-fitting black garment clung to her like a second skin, leaving little to the imagination. The smooth texture of the latex teased her own senses, amplifying her desire to dominate and control.

As Nurse Cassandra stood beside Mark, her latex-gloved hand reached out to gently stroke his cheek. Mark's breath hitched at the touch, his eyes locked on hers, pleading for permission to surrender. His submission fueled her desire, and she relished in the power she held over him.

"Are you ready, Mark?" she purred, her voice a velvety whisper that sent shivers down his spine. Mark nodded, his voice caught in his throat, unable to articulate his need for the latex restraints that Nurse Cassandra promised.

Wordlessly, Nurse Cassandra moved to a nearby cabinet, her latex-clad body swaying gracefully with every step. She retrieved a collection of sleek, black latex straps, each one designed to securely bind Mark's limbs. Returning to his side, she held the restraints in front of him, allowing him to see the intricate buckles and shiny surface that would encase his body.

With a hint of anticipation in her eyes, Nurse Cassandra gave Mark a seductive smile before instructing him to spread his arms wide. As he complied, she took one strap and began to wrap it around his left wrist, the coolness of the latex making his skin tingle. She fastened the buckle tightly, ensuring that he would be securely restrained.

With the left wrist secure, Nurse Cassandra moved to his right, repeating the process with meticulous care. The intimate act of binding Mark in latex restraints sent waves of pleasure through her own body, heightening her arousal. Each click of the buckle resonated with the growing tension between them.

As Nurse Cassandra admired her handiwork, she could see the mixture of apprehension and excitement in Mark's eyes. The sight fueled her dominance, and she craved more control. Without a word, she moved to the end of the examination table, her latex-clad body gliding effortlessly.

"Spread your legs for me, Mark," she commanded, her voice laced with authority. Mark obeyed, parting his legs, exposing his vulnerability. His breath quickened, the anticipation making his heart race. He trusted Nurse Cassandra implicitly, knowing she would push his limits while keeping him safe.

Nurse Cassandra retrieved two additional latex straps and, with practiced precision, secured them around Mark's ankles. The sound of the buckles tightening echoed in the room, heightening the tension between them. She admired her work, relishing in the sight of her submissive patient completely at her mercy, his body bound in latex.

"Now, Mark, you are completely under my control," Nurse Cassandra declared, her voice commanding. "You have surrendered yourself to the latex restraints, and I will ensure your utmost pleasure and satisfaction."

Mark's eyes were filled with a mixture of desire and trust as he gazed up at Nurse Cassandra. The power she possessed was intoxicating, igniting a fire within him that he had never experienced before. He was ready to embrace the sensations that awaited him.

With slow, deliberate movements, Nurse Cassandra circled the examination table, running her latex-gloved fingertips along Mark's exposed skin. Goose bumps erupted in their wake, a physical testament to the power of her touch. Mark quivered with anticipation, his body responding to the erotic energy that crackled in the air.

Leaning over him, Nurse Cassandra lowered her face to his, her lips hovering just inches away from his ear. Her breath, warm and tinged with desire, caressed his skin.

"Prepare yourself, Mark," she whispered, her voice a sultry promise. "The true exploration of pleasure begins now, bound in latex, under my complete control."

As the words hung in the air, the room embraced them, morphing into a sanctuary where their desires intertwined. Nurse Cassandra, the embodiment of dominance and sensuality, was about to take Mark on a journey he would never forget—a journey where the boundaries of pleasure would be pushed to their limits, and the latex restraints would bind them together in an intoxicating dance of submission and ecstasy.

Chapter 5: The Discipline Session

Nurse Cassandra, her vibrant red hair cascading in loose waves around her shoulders, led Mark into the dimly lit chamber adjacent to the Latex Ward. The room was adorned with an assortment of implements, all meticulously arranged, promising both pleasure and pain. The air crackled with anticipation as the soft glow of subdued lighting cast shadows across the latex-covered walls.

Mark's heart raced as he took in the sight before him—the dominating presence of Nurse Cassandra in her skin-tight latex uniform, her eyes gleaming with a mixture of authority and desire. She exuded an irresistible power that sent shivers down his spine, igniting a fire within him that yearned to be tamed.

"Undress," she commanded, her voice low and commanding, as she leaned against a table adorned with an array of paddles and floggers. Mark's hands trembled slightly as he complied, his every movement eager to please the alluring nurse. Piece by piece, his clothes fell to the floor, leaving him bare and vulnerable, exposed to her watchful gaze.

Nurse Cassandra circled him like a predator, her eyes tracing every inch of his body, assessing his readiness for the impending discipline. Her latex-clad fingertips brushed against his skin, sending electric currents of desire coursing through his veins. The soft, cool touch of the rubber against his heated flesh only fueled his anticipation.

"Kneel," she commanded, her voice resonating with authority. Mark obeyed, sinking to his knees on the padded floor, his eyes fixated on her every move. She picked up a small latex paddle, testing its weight in her hand before walking towards him, her heels clicking on the polished floor. As she approached, he could feel the intensity of the moment building, like a crescendo of desire ready to explode.

With a flick of her wrist, Nurse Cassandra delivered the first strike, the paddle meeting Mark's exposed flesh with a resounding thud. A jolt of pain mixed with pleasure surged through his body, causing him to gasp. Each subsequent strike landed with deliberate precision, alternating between stinging slaps and gentle taps that stirred his senses.

Mark's breath became ragged, his body absorbing the sensation of the latex paddle against his skin, each impact leaving a mark that reminded him of his submission. Nurse Cassandra watched him intently, her gaze unwavering, attuned to his every reaction. She knew when to push him to the edge, testing the boundaries of his endurance, and when to offer him a moment of respite.

As the discipline session progressed, Nurse Cassandra's movements became a seductive dance, a symphony of dominance and submission. She seamlessly transitioned from the latex paddle to a leather flogger, its long, supple strands gliding across Mark's sensitized flesh. Each strike sent waves of pleasurable agony coursing through him, his body arching instinctively to meet the delicious pain.

But it wasn't just the physical sensations that consumed Mark—it was the undeniable connection he felt with Nurse Cassandra. Each strike was an affirmation of trust, a testament to their shared desires and mutual exploration. In her presence, he discovered a freedom he had longed for, a liberation from societal constraints that allowed him to embrace his true self.

As the session neared its climax, Nurse Cassandra delivered a final, decisive strike, the impact resonating through Mark's body like a thunderclap. His vision blurred, his senses heightened, and a primal scream escaped his lips as he succumbed to the cathartic release that coursed through his veins. The intensity of the moment left him trembling, his body awash with a potent cocktail of pleasure, pain, and surrender.

Nurse Cassandra, her commanding aura momentarily softened, knelt before him, her gloved hand tenderly caressing his cheek. "You've done well, my dear," she whispered, her voice a soothing balm against the storm within him. She helped him rise, supporting him as his legs wobbled from the sheer intensity of the experience.

As they stood together, Nurse Cassandra's gaze held a gentle reassurance, a silent promise of aftercare to come. She led Mark to a nearby chaise longue, draped in plush latex cushions, and guided him to lie down. Slowly, she began to unfasten his restraints, the act a tender ritual of release and trust.

With the discipline session complete, Nurse Cassandra settled beside him, her presence a comforting embrace. She whispered words of affirmation, her fingertips tracing soothing circles on his skin, as they both descended from the heights of their shared journey. In that moment of vulnerability and intimacy, they found solace in one another's arms, knowing that their connection transcended the confines of the Latex Ward.

And as they basked in the afterglow of their shared exploration, Nurse Cassandra and Mark reveled in the profound bond they had forged—one that continued to ignite their desires, pushing the boundaries of their own understanding of pleasure, pain, and the power of surrender.

Chapter 6: The Aftercare

Nurse Cassandra tenderly unfastened the last of the latex restraints, allowing Mark to stretch his limbs and regain his freedom. His body, marked with red welts from the disciplinary session, bore witness to the intensity of their encounter. As the last echoes of pleasure faded, Nurse Cassandra transitioned seamlessly into her nurturing role, her emerald eyes filled with a compassionate warmth.

She reached out a delicate hand to brush away a few strands of her short red hair that had fallen across her face. Her fingertips traced a soothing path down Mark's cheek, a gesture that spoke of understanding and care. "How are you feeling, my dear?" she asked, her voice a soft caress in the dimly lit room.

Mark, still basking in the euphoric haze of their shared experience, struggled to find his words. His gaze locked onto Nurse Cassandra's, captivated by her unwavering presence and the genuine concern etched upon her flawless features. "I... I'm feeling a mixture of emotions, Nurse Cassandra," he finally admitted, his voice tinged with vulnerability.

She smiled, a tender curve of her lips that spoke volumes of reassurance. "That's perfectly normal, Mark. What we shared here was intense, both physically and emotionally. It's important to acknowledge and process those emotions." Nurse Cassandra moved closer, her latex-clad body radiating comfort as she settled beside him on the plush, velvet-covered chaise longue.

Leaning against her, Mark allowed himself to be enveloped in her warm embrace, feeling the smoothness of the latex against his bare skin. Nurse Cassandra's nimble fingers trailed lightly along his arm, leaving a trail of tingling sensations in their wake. Her touch was both soothing and electrifying, a potent combination that stirred something deep within him.

"Nurse Cassandra," he whispered, his voice laden with a mix of gratitude and desire. "Thank you for guiding me through this journey, for showing me a side of myself I never knew existed."

Her gentle laughter danced through the room, like a melody that set his heart ablaze. "You're very welcome, Mark. It's my privilege to guide and nurture those who seek the unexplored depths of their desires. Trust is the cornerstone of what we do here, and your trust in me is a gift."

Mark turned to face her fully, his eyes locked onto hers. His hand reached out, hesitating for a moment before finding its place on her cheek, his touch reverent. "Nurse Cassandra, there's something about you... something extraordinary that draws me to you. It's more than just the latex and the role you embody. It's you, as a person. Your compassion, your strength, your presence."

Nurse Cassandra's emerald eyes shimmered with a mixture of vulnerability and longing. She leaned into his touch, her breath hitching ever so slightly. "Mark, you have a profound effect on me as well. It takes a special kind of person to embrace the duality of dominance and vulnerability, to understand the intricacies of power and surrender. And in you, I find that person."

Their gazes locked in a silent understanding, the air between them thick with unspoken desires. Nurse Cassandra's hand found its way to Mark's chest, feeling the steady beat of his heart beneath her fingertips. "But for now, my dear, let us focus on your aftercare," she murmured, her voice laced with a gentle command.

With practiced tenderness, Nurse Cassandra guided Mark to recline on the chaise longue, his body sinking into the luxurious cushions. She knelt beside him, her latex-clad knees brushing against the fabric of his pants, and began to work her skilled hands over his weary muscles. Her touch was both firm and soothing, expertly easing away the residual tension that lingered.

As her hands moved across his body, Mark felt himself surrendering to her care completely, his mind and body attuned to her every touch. Nurse Cassandra's attention was focused solely on him, her movements deliberate and purposeful. It was as if time had ceased to exist, leaving only the intoxicating connection between them.

Her hands eventually reached his shoulders, strong yet delicate as they kneaded away the knots of tension that had built up during their session. Mark let out a sigh of relief, surrendering to the profound sense of release that accompanied Nurse Cassandra's ministrations.

The room was filled with a symphony of their breathing, the rustle of latex, and the occasional whispered word of comfort. Mark's eyelids grew heavy as the combined effects of their intense encounter and Nurse Cassandra's skilled aftercare lulled him into a state of blissful relaxation.

As Nurse Cassandra continued to work her magic, her hands gliding across his skin with an almost ethereal grace, she leaned in closer. Her breath brushed against his ear, sending shivers of anticipation down his spine. "Mark, remember that what we shared here is a sacred trust," she murmured, her voice laden with a mixture of affection and authority. "It's an experience that will forever be etched in our memories. Whenever you need to revisit this realm of exploration, know that I am here for you."

Mark nodded, his mind and body in perfect synchrony with the woman who had unveiled his deepest desires. "I will remember, Nurse Cassandra. You have opened a door within me, and I am forever changed."

A soft smile graced Nurse Cassandra's lips as she continued her gentle caresses, her touch serving as a balm for his soul. In that moment, as the room pulsed with intimacy and vulnerability, they both understood that their connection went far beyond the latex-clad encounters of the Latex Ward. It was a connection that defied convention, transcending the bounds of their roles, and finding solace in the uncharted territories of their hearts.

Together, they lingered in the afterglow of their shared experience, lost in a world where latex, desire, and tender care merged into something beautiful and profound. And as the minutes slipped away, Nurse Cassandra and Mark relished in the knowledge that their journey had only just begun, fueled by an unspoken promise of exploration, trust, and an unwavering connection that defied the confines of the Latex Ward.

Latex Training Academy

Chapter 1: Enrollment

Rebecca nervously stood outside the ornate gates of the Latex Training Academy, her heart pounding in her chest. The building itself exuded an air of mystery and intrigue, with its sleek, modern architecture and a touch of seductive elegance. It was as if the academy itself was beckoning her, inviting her to explore the hidden desires she had long kept locked away.

With a trembling hand, she reached for the academy's polished brass door handle, feeling the cool metal against her skin. As she stepped inside, a wave of anticipation washed over her. The reception area was tastefully adorned with black and red accents, exuding an aura of dominance and sensuality. A well-dressed receptionist greeted her with a knowing smile, her eyes lingering on Rebecca's attire.

Rebecca, a striking young woman in her mid-twenties, possessed an alluring beauty that often drew the attention of others. Her silky chestnut hair cascaded in loose waves around her shoulders, framing a face adorned with mesmerizing green eyes and soft, full lips that held a hint of mystery. There was an air of innocence about her, but beneath the surface, a fiery passion smoldered, waiting to be unleashed.

Today, she had carefully selected her outfit, seeking a balance between professionalism and allure. She wore a fitted white blouse that accentuated her curves, the buttons straining against the gentle swell of her ample bosom. The blouse was tucked into a knee-length black pencil skirt, hugging her shapely hips and accentuating her slender waist. A pair of high-heeled black pumps completed the ensemble, elongating her legs and giving her an undeniable air of confidence.

Rebecca had always possessed an affinity for latex, the way it clung to her body, embracing every curve and contour. The thought of wearing it filled her with a delicious sense of anticipation. As she stood there, waiting for her turn to be called, she imagined the feel of the smooth, sleek material against her skin, igniting a spark deep within her.

Finally, her name was called, and she was led down a long corridor that seemed to whisper secrets in every flickering light. The clicking of her heels on the polished marble floor echoed through the hallway, amplifying her excitement and apprehension. She could hardly believe she was about to embark on a journey that would merge her love for nursing with her hidden desires.

Entering a lavishly decorated room, she found herself face-to-face with Mistress Victoria, the head instructor of the academy. Mistress Victoria exuded an air of authority and confidence, her presence commanding attention. Dressed in a form-fitting latex bodysuit that accentuated her every curve, she exuded power and sensuality in equal measure. Her raven-black hair cascaded over her shoulders, contrasting against the sheen of her skin-tight latex attire.

Mistress Victoria's piercing hazel eyes locked onto Rebecca's, seemingly peering into the depths of her soul. There was an unspoken understanding between them, a recognition of shared desires. As they exchanged pleasantries, Rebecca found herself captivated by the Mistress's magnetic presence, unable to tear her gaze away from the woman who held the key to her deepest fantasies.

The conversation flowed effortlessly as Mistress Victoria delved into Rebecca's motivations, her desires, and her experiences. With each word, Rebecca felt a growing connection, a sense of acceptance she had never felt before. It was as if she had finally found a place where her desires could be embraced and nurtured.

As the interview drew to a close, Mistress Victoria leaned forward, her voice low and seductive. "Rebecca, I see the fire burning within you. The Latex Training Academy can help you embrace your desires, explore the boundaries of pleasure, and merge your passion for nursing with the world of dominance and submission. Should you choose to embark on this journey, be prepared for a transformation like no other."

Rebecca's heart raced at the Mistress's words, her mind awash with possibilities. She knew deep down that this was her chance to discover the woman she truly was, to shed the restraints of societal expectations and embrace her sensual nature. With a firm nod, she accepted the Mistress's offer, a surge of excitement coursing through her veins.

As she left the room, Rebecca knew that her life was about to change forever. She was ready to immerse herself in the world of latex, dominance, and medical expertise—a world that promised pleasure, discovery, and a liberation of her deepest desires.

Chapter 2: Dressing the Part

Rebecca nervously entered the dressing room, her heart pounding with anticipation. The room was a haven of sensuality, with walls adorned with mirrors reflecting the dimly lit space. Racks of latex uniforms lined the walls, a vivid spectrum of colors and styles beckoning her closer. The air carried a faint scent of rubber, mingling with an undercurrent of desire.

Mistress Victoria, the enigmatic head instructor of the Latex Training Academy, stood at the center of the room. Her presence commanded attention, radiating an aura of confidence and dominance. Her shapely figure was accentuated by the tight embrace of a black latex corset, cinching her waist and emphasizing her curves. Her legs, encased in sheer black stockings, led to stiletto heels that completed the seductive ensemble.

Rebecca's gaze wandered over Mistress Victoria's attire, a mixture of awe and longing building within her. She marveled at how the sleek latex seemed to mold perfectly to her form, hugging every contour with an almost supernatural precision. The material shone under the soft lighting, a glossy sheen that amplified its inherent allure. A subtle flush crept onto Rebecca's cheeks as she imagined herself dressed in such provocative elegance.

Mistress Victoria turned her gaze towards Rebecca, her eyes locked onto the younger woman's. There was a moment of intense connection, a silent understanding passing between them. Without uttering a word, Mistress

Victoria began guiding Rebecca through the transformative process of dressing in latex.

Rebecca's body tingled with anticipation as Mistress Victoria selected a crimson latex nurse's uniform from the rack. The color seemed to pulsate with vitality, reflecting her own burgeoning desire to explore this seductive world. She felt the smooth texture of the latex against her fingertips, sending a shiver down her spine. The dress was form-fitting, accentuating her curves and cinching her waist with a built-in corset. The neckline dipped teasingly, hinting at the lushness of her cleavage.

Mistress Victoria's skilled hands glided over Rebecca's body as she assisted her in donning the garment. Their touch was electrifying, igniting a fire within Rebecca that she had never experienced before. The latex clung to her skin like a second, sensual layer, heightening her awareness of every inch of her body.

As Rebecca stood before the mirror, she hardly recognized herself. The crimson latex nurse's uniform transformed her, empowering her with a newfound confidence and allure. Her dark hair cascaded down her shoulders, framing her face, which was flushed with a mixture of excitement and trepidation. Her eyes sparkled with a mix of curiosity and desire, reflecting the journey she had embarked upon.

Mistress Victoria stepped back, her gaze appraising Rebecca with satisfaction. "You look absolutely stunning," she purred, her voice dripping with approval. "The latex has embraced your body, becoming an extension of your desires. You are a vision of power and sensuality."

Rebecca's heart swelled with pride, her inhibitions melting away in the face of Mistress Victoria's affirmation. In this latex-clad world, she had found a place where her passions and desires could thrive, unencumbered by societal expectations. The material that adorned her body was more than just clothing; it was a symbol of her liberation and the exploration of her deepest desires.

With newfound confidence coursing through her veins, Rebecca embraced her reflection. She twirled and swayed, reveling in the sensual embrace of the latex. The fabric whispered against her skin, a symphony of desire that echoed in her ears. In that moment, she knew that she had found her calling – to embody the dominatrix nurse, commanding respect and desire in equal measure.

As Rebecca and Mistress Victoria stood side by side, both adorned in latex, the air crackled with an electric energy. They were kindred spirits, united by their shared love for the material and the intoxicating power it bestowed upon them. Together, they would explore the boundaries of latex and dominance, unlocking the secrets of this alluring realm.

In the dressing room, where their journey had begun, Rebecca's transformation was complete. She had embraced her desires, surrendering to the seductive allure of latex. And with each passing moment, the world of the Latex Training Academy beckoned her further, promising encounters that would push the boundaries of pleasure and self-discovery.

As the door closed behind them, Rebecca took a deep breath, ready to step into a world where latex and desire intertwined, where the lines between pleasure and pain blurred. And with Mistress Victoria by her side, she knew that this journey would be an awakening, an exploration of her deepest fantasies that would forever change the course of her life.

Chapter 3: Anatomy Lessons

Rebecca's heart raced as she stepped into the training room, the scent of latex enveloping her senses. Mistress Victoria, her mentor and instructor, stood tall and commanding, dressed in a figure-hugging latex outfit that accentuated every curve of her body. Her jet-black hair cascaded over her shoulders, and her piercing gaze held an undeniable allure.

Rebecca couldn't help but admire Mistress Victoria's confidence and poise, her every movement exuding dominance and sensuality. It was clear that she had mastered the art of blending medical expertise with the provocative nature of latex. Rebecca yearned to follow in her footsteps, to embody that same commanding presence.

As they entered the training room, Rebecca took in the sight before her. Shelves were lined with an array of medical equipment, meticulously arranged and ready for use. A medical examination table, covered in black latex, stood at the center of the room, inviting both vulnerability and anticipation. The air crackled with a potent mix of excitement and trepidation.

Mistress Victoria's eyes locked with Rebecca's, a silent understanding passing between them. She beckoned Rebecca forward, her voice low and commanding. "Come, my dear. Let us explore the delicate dance of dominance and submission within the realm of medical examinations."

Rebecca approached, feeling the subtle brush of Mistress Victoria's latex-clad hand against her arm, sending shivers of anticipation through her body. Her mentor's touch awakened something deep within her, igniting a fire that burned brightly, demanding to be explored.

Mistress Victoria guided Rebecca towards the examination table, the latex material cool against her fingertips. "First, my dear, we must ensure that the patient feels secure and submissive," she murmured, her voice laced with authority. "We shall begin by applying restraints."

Rebecca's heart pounded with a mixture of apprehension and excitement as Mistress Victoria demonstrated the art of skillful restraint. The sound of the cuffs clicking shut, snug against the patient's wrists, echoed in the room. The vulnerability and surrender evident in the patient's eyes heightened the intensity of the moment.

"Now, observe closely, my dear," Mistress Victoria said, her voice a potent combination of reassurance and command. "Every touch, every movement is an opportunity to exert control and evoke pleasure."

Rebecca watched intently as Mistress Victoria's hands expertly maneuvered across the patient's body. With precision and grace, she performed various medical examinations, incorporating the aesthetics of latex with the power dynamics of dominance and submission. Her gloved hands glided effortlessly over the patient's skin, instilling a sense of both vulnerability and safety.

As Mistress Victoria continued her demonstration, Rebecca's mind began to wander. She imagined herself in the role of the dominant nurse, dressed in a latex uniform that hugged her every curve, accentuating her confidence and allure. She pictured the way the latex would cling to her body, the way it would make her feel powerful and desirable.

Her thoughts were interrupted as Mistress Victoria's voice cut through the haze of her daydream. "Rebecca, my dear, it is now your turn. Show me what you have learned."

Rebecca's heart skipped a beat, a mixture of nerves and excitement coursing through her veins. With trembling hands, she donned a pair of latex gloves, feeling the smooth material against her skin. Taking a deep breath, she stepped forward, ready to embrace her newfound role as the dominant nurse.

As Rebecca performed her first examination, she realized that her journey was just beginning. The fusion of latex and dominance held an intoxicating allure, and she longed to explore it further, to push the boundaries of pleasure and control.

With each movement, each touch, Rebecca embraced her own power and desire.

She discovered the unique satisfaction that came from blending medical expertise with the seductive allure of latex. Under Mistress Victoria's watchful gaze, Rebecca blossomed, her confidence growing with every examination.

Rebecca knew that her path had been forever altered. The world of latex and dominance had become her playground, a realm where she could explore the depths of her desires and find a new level of fulfillment. And with Mistress Victoria as her guide, she was determined to excel in the art of anatomy, both medical and erotic, that would define her journey as a dominatrix nurse dressed in the alluring embrace of latex.

Chapter 4: Psychological Dominance

Rebecca's heart raced as she entered the lecture hall, her eyes scanning the room for Mistress Victoria. Her mentor, the epitome of seductive power, was already perched on a raised platform at the front, exuding an air of confidence that commanded attention. Rebecca's breath hitched as she took in the sight before her.

Mistress Victoria, with her lustrous raven locks cascading down her back, was dressed in a form-fitting latex corset that accentuated her hourglass figure. The corset clung to her curves, emphasizing her ample bosom and cinching her waist, enhancing her dominion over the room. The latex shimmered with a deep, enchanting black hue that whispered secrets of desire and dominance.

As Rebecca settled into her seat, she couldn't help but be captivated by Mistress Victoria's attire. It was a bold proclamation of her dominance, a visual testament to her authority. The corset was accompanied by a tight-fitting latex skirt that molded to her hips, outlining the enticing contours of her body. Her long, slender legs were sheathed in thigh-high latex boots, each step she took commanding attention and admiration.

The lecture began, and Mistress Victoria's voice, velvety and intoxicating, filled the room. Her words carried a magnetic power that held the students in rapt attention. Rebecca found herself mesmerized by the interplay of Mistress Victoria's voice, her commanding presence, and the tantalizing allure of the latex garments that adorned her.

As the lecture progressed, Mistress Victoria delved deeper into the psychological aspects of dominance. Her knowledge and experience flowed effortlessly, filling Rebecca's mind with a mixture of fascination and curiosity. She explored the art of verbal control, teaching the students how to wield words as weapons, expertly crafting commands that evoked obedience and desire.

Rebecca found herself enthralled by the subtleties of psychological dominance. She yearned to master this skill, to understand the intricate dance between power and submission, to have her patients hanging on her every word. Mistress Victoria's guidance was pivotal in helping her unravel these intricacies.

After the lecture, Mistress Victoria requested Rebecca's presence in her private office. Nervously, Rebecca followed, her mind buzzing with anticipation and a hint of trepidation. She wondered what Mistress Victoria had in store for her, what further depths of her desires would be uncovered.

Entering the office, Rebecca was greeted by an intimate space adorned with dark red velvet curtains and low ambient lighting. The air was infused with a heady blend of incense, heightening the senses and adding an aura of mystique to the room. Mistress Victoria motioned for Rebecca to sit on a plush, velvet-covered chair, her eyes glittering with both warmth and authority.

"Rebecca," Mistress Victoria purred, her voice rich with a hint of amusement, "Today, we shall explore the power of your voice and how it can unravel the deepest recesses of a submissive's desires."

Rebecca's cheeks flushed, her heart pounding in her chest. She felt a mixture of excitement and nervousness, a delicious cocktail of sensations that fueled her anticipation. Mistress Victoria stood up, gracefully moving towards a small table adorned with an array of objects. Her fingers danced over the items, finally selecting a sleek, black microphone.

With a flick of her wrist, Mistress Victoria gestured for Rebecca to approach. "Take this microphone, my dear, and explore the intoxicating power of your voice. I want you to create a scenario where you command obedience, ignite desire, and leave your submissive craving more."

Rebecca's hands trembled slightly as she accepted the microphone. She held it close to her lips, feeling its coolness against her skin. Taking a deep breath, she closed her eyes and let her voice take control.

"In a room enveloped in darkness, you stand before me, stripped of all defenses. Every fiber of your being yearns to obey my every command. Your mind is a blank canvas, waiting for my words to paint vivid scenes of desire and surrender. With each syllable that escapes my lips, your pulse quickens, your breath becomes shallow. I am the mistress of your desires, and you are my devoted servant."

As the words spilled forth, Rebecca felt a surge of confidence. The power of her voice reverberated through the room, weaving a spell of dominance and submission. Mistress Victoria watched with a glimmer of pride and satisfaction, recognizing the blossoming dominance within Rebecca.

Time seemed to stand still as Rebecca's voice painted intricate images of passion and servitude. She explored the depths of her imagination, creating scenarios that tantalized and teased. The microphone became an extension of her desires, amplifying her words and granting them a tangible presence.

When she finally paused, Rebecca's eyes fluttered open, meeting Mistress Victoria's gaze. The room was charged with an electric energy, a potent blend of dominance and surrender. Mistress Victoria's smile was both approving and intoxicating, acknowledging the progress Rebecca had made in embracing her dominant nature.

"Bravo, my dear," Mistress Victoria murmured, her voice laced with admiration. "Your journey into dominance has just begun, and your voice will become a formidable weapon in your arsenal. Remember, dominance lies not only in the attire we wear but also in the power we command with our words."

As Rebecca left the office that day, she carried with her a newfound confidence and a deeper understanding of the intricate dance between dominance and submission. She knew that her journey at the Latex Training Academy was far from over, and with each passing encounter, she would continue to embrace her role as a dominatrix nurse, draped in latex, exuding power and passion.

Chapter 5: The Ward Experience

Rebecca stood outside the door to the Latex Ward, anticipation coursing through her veins. Dressed in a form-fitting latex nurse uniform, its glossy surface clung to her curves like a second skin. Her raven-black hair cascaded down her back, contrasting against the pristine white color of the uniform. She adjusted the tight corset, accentuating her hourglass figure and enhancing her natural allure. With every step, the sound of her high-heeled boots echoed through the hallway, announcing her arrival.

As she entered the ward, the scent of latex enveloped her, heightening her senses and intensifying the atmosphere. The room was dimly lit, with soft ambient lighting casting a seductive glow over the medical equipment and restraints adorning the walls. The sound of faint moans and whispers filled the air, mingling with the rustling of latex.

Mistress Victoria, the head instructor, stood at the center of the ward, her commanding presence drawing everyone's attention. Dressed in a provocative latex nurse ensemble, she exuded confidence and power. Her emerald-green eyes sparkled mischievously, promising a journey of pleasure and pain. Rebecca couldn't help but be captivated by her elegance and authority.

Mistress Victoria approached Rebecca, her gaze raking over her latex-clad body. "Rebecca, welcome to the Latex Ward," she purred, her voice laced with a seductive undertone. "Today, you will have the opportunity to experience the delicate balance between medical care and submission."

Rebecca nodded, her heart pounding in her chest. She was eager to explore this unique realm and embrace her dominant side fully. Mistress Victoria led her to a private room, where a patient, clad in a latex catsuit and bound to the examination table, awaited their attentions.

"Meet Matthew," Mistress Victoria introduced him, a glint of excitement in her eyes. "He desires a mix of medical procedures and sensual dominance. Your task is to administer his treatments while maintaining control."

Rebecca approached Matthew, her mind focused and her movements deliberate. She relished the authority that came with being a dominatrix nurse. Her latex gloves, slick and cool against her skin, hinted at the tactile pleasure to come. With a gentle touch, she traced her gloved fingers along Matthew's exposed flesh, relishing the shivers of anticipation that coursed through his body.

Mistress Victoria observed from a distance, offering guidance and encouragement when needed. As Rebecca donned a pair of latex cuffs, she secured Matthew's wrists to the examination table, ensuring his compliance and vulnerability. The control she exerted was as intoxicating to her as it was to him.

With calculated precision, Rebecca performed a range of medical procedures, combining them seamlessly with tantalizing caresses and whispered commands. Each touch and sensation heightened the intensity of the experience, blurring the lines between pain and pleasure. Matthew's muffled moans mingled with Rebecca's soft-spoken reassurances, creating a symphony of desire within the confines of the ward.

Rebecca's confidence grew with every passing moment. She reveled in her ability to navigate the delicate balance between caring for Matthew's well-being and fueling his submissive desires. Her own arousal pulsed through her, the sensuality of the latex uniform heightening her senses and deepening her connection to the experience.

Mistress Victoria observed with a knowing smile, acknowledging Rebecca's growth and her natural talent for this unique form of domination. Under her mentor's guidance, Rebecca discovered her true power as a dominatrix nurse—a power that extended beyond physical control to the emotional and psychological realms.

As the session drew to a close, Rebecca carefully released Matthew from his restraints, her touch tender yet commanding. She offered him a moment to recover, her presence a comforting anchor in the midst of his surrender. With a nod of approval from Mistress Victoria, Rebecca left the room, her heart brimming with exhilaration and a newfound sense of purpose.

In that moment, Rebecca realized that being a dominatrix nurse in latex was more than just a fantasy—it was a calling. The fusion of medical care, dominance, and the provocative allure of latex awakened something within her—a force she was ready to embrace fully. As she walked away from the Latex Ward, her body humming with desire, she knew that this was just the beginning of her journey into a world where pleasure and healing intertwined in the most decadent of ways.

Chapter 6: Graduation

Rebecca stood before the mirrored wall of the Latex Training Academy, her heart pounding with a mix of excitement and anticipation. Her journey through the academy had been a whirlwind of self-discovery and exploration, and now, she was on the cusp of achieving her goal: becoming a certified dominatrix nurse skilled in the art of latex. The final assessment awaited her, a make-or-break moment that would determine her fate.

Taking a deep breath, Rebecca admired her reflection. She had transformed during her time at the academy, not just in terms of knowledge and skills but also in her confidence and self-assuredness. Her once shy demeanor had given way to a captivating aura, one that commanded attention and respect. Her hazel eyes sparkled with a newfound determination, while her luscious chestnut hair cascaded down her back, framing her delicate features.

As the academy's dress code dictated, Rebecca wore a stunning latex ensemble, carefully selected for this significant occasion. The figure-hugging black catsuit clung to her curves like a second skin, accentuating her slender waist and ample bosom. The high collar emphasized the graceful length of her neck, while the long, fitted sleeves accentuated her toned arms. The suit seamlessly blended elegance and eroticism, a testament to her growth as a dominatrix nurse.

Completing her attire, Rebecca adorned herself with black latex gloves, reaching just below her elbows. Their smooth surface sent shivers of anticipation up her arms, a tangible reminder of the power she held within her grasp. Her matching thigh-high latex boots added a touch of dominance to her ensemble, their shiny surface reflecting the ambient light in the room.

With a final glance in the mirror, Rebecca adjusted her attire, ensuring every detail was impeccable. She had learned during her training that presentation was key— an outward display of confidence and authority. And as she stood there, dressed in latex from head to toe, she embodied the epitome of dominance, ready to prove her worth and passion.

The doors to the assessment room swung open, and Mistress Victoria, the head instructor, stepped out, her presence commanding attention. Clad in a striking red latex ensemble, she exuded an air of dominance that left no doubt as to her expertise. Her penetrating gaze met Rebecca's, a mixture of pride and expectation shining through.

"Rebecca," Mistress Victoria's voice resonated with authority, "it's time for your final assessment. Are you ready to showcase what you've learned during your time here?"

Rebecca straightened her posture, her heart pounding against her chest. She took a deep breath, her voice steady but filled with determination. "Yes, Mistress Victoria. I am ready."

As they entered the assessment room, Rebecca's eyes widened at the sight before her. It was an elaborately designed space, carefully arranged to simulate a medical facility, complete with various pieces of equipment and furniture. The room was dimly lit, casting an ethereal glow upon the scene.

Mistress Victoria led Rebecca to a sturdy examination table covered in glossy latex. "Today, you will demonstrate your mastery of both medical expertise and the art of dominance. You will conduct a complete examination of our volunteer patient, ensuring their physical well-being while simultaneously indulging their desires."

Rebecca nodded, her mind sharp and focused. She approached the patient, who lay partially restrained on the table, their eyes filled with anticipation and trust. They wore nothing but a thin layer of latex, their body glistening under the soft light.

Taking a moment to collect herself, Rebecca donned a pair of latex gloves, the cool material sending a jolt of excitement through her fingertips. She began with a thorough assessment, her hands moving with precision and confidence. The patient's heartbeat raced beneath her touch, their breath hitching with each careful examination.

Rebecca skillfully combined her medical knowledge with sensual caresses, navigating the fine line between pleasure and care. She listened attentively to the patient's desires, adapting her approach to meet their needs, all the while maintaining an unwavering dominance that left them yearning for more.

The examination flowed seamlessly, with Rebecca showcasing her expertise in a symphony of touch, control, and connection. The room was filled with moans of pleasure and whispers of satisfaction, the air heavy with an undeniable tension.

As she concluded the examination, Rebecca stepped back, her gaze filled with a mixture of triumph and satisfaction. She had accomplished what she set out to do—merge the world of latex, dominance, and medical expertise into a harmonious and fulfilling experience.

Mistress Victoria approached, her expression a mix of pride and admiration. "Rebecca, you have surpassed our expectations. Your journey through the academy has transformed you into a remarkable dominatrix nurse. Today, we celebrate your graduation."

A surge of joy and accomplishment washed over Rebecca as Mistress Victoria bestowed upon her a certification, signifying her success. Tears welled in her eyes as she accepted the honor, her voice quivering with gratitude. "Thank you, Mistress Victoria. I am forever grateful for the guidance and knowledge you have imparted upon me."

As she held her certification in her hands, Rebecca knew that her journey had only just begun. Armed with her newfound skills and adorned in the captivating allure of latex, she was ready to embark on a path that would intertwine pleasure, care, and dominance. The Latex Training Academy had shaped her into a formidable force—a dominatrix nurse who would leave an indelible mark on those who dared to explore the boundaries of their desires.

The Latex Asylum

Chapter 1: The Intake Assessment

Mistress Victoria, the dominatrix nurse of the Latex Asylum, possessed an irresistible allure that left her patients mesmerized. With her raven-black hair cascading down her back, contrasting against her fair complexion, she exuded an enigmatic beauty. Her piercing green eyes held a glint of mischief, promising both pleasure and pain to those who crossed her path.

As she walked through the hallowed halls of the Latex Asylum, every step carried an air of confidence and authority. Her figure was adorned in a form-fitting latex nurse uniform, the glossy material molding to her curves like a second skin. The uniform's plunging neckline teased a glimpse of her ample cleavage, and the strategically placed zippers hinted at the tantalizing delights that lay beneath the smooth latex surface.

Mistress Victoria reveled in the power her attire bestowed upon her. The feel of the latex against her skin ignited a fire within, amplifying her dominant nature. It was more than just a uniform; it was an embodiment of her control and the visual representation of the desires she was about to unlock within her patients.

She entered the room where Edward anxiously awaited his assessment. The dimly lit space was adorned with black leather furniture and a single spotlight focused on a padded examination table. The scent of latex lingered in the air, mingling with a hint of vanilla, an intentional sensory fusion that set the stage for the encounter.

Edward's eyes widened as Mistress Victoria entered, her presence commanding attention. His gaze traveled from the top of her latex-clad head down to her black stiletto heels, taking in every curve and contour. He found himself drawn to the way the material clung to her body, emphasizing her feminine form in all the right places.

"Welcome to the Latex Asylum, Edward," she purred, her voice like velvet, coaxing him deeper into her web of dominance. Her eyes, a vibrant shade of green, locked onto his, holding him captive. "Tell me, what brings you to seek treatment here?"

Edward swallowed, his voice catching in his throat. "I... I've always had these... desires," he stammered, his face flushing with a mix of embarrassment and anticipation. "I've struggled to reconcile them with my everyday life, and it's consuming me."

Mistress Victoria nodded, her latex-gloved fingers gracefully brushing her lips as she listened intently. "You're not alone, Edward," she said, her voice laced with empathy. "Many of our patients come here seeking solace and understanding for their desires. The Latex Asylum is a sanctuary, a place where we embrace and explore the depths of our desires without judgment."

As she spoke, her fingers idly traced the zipper on her uniform, a subtle gesture that didn't go unnoticed by Edward. His eyes followed the path of her touch, his mind aflame with the possibilities that lay ahead.

"I'm here to guide you through this journey, Edward," Mistress Victoria continued, her tone a delicate balance of authority and reassurance. "Together, we will delve into your desires, untangle the knots in your mind, and liberate you from the burden of societal expectations. Are you ready to surrender to your true self?"

Edward's heart pounded in his chest as he met her gaze once again. He knew that this encounter would be a turning point in his life, a step towards embracing the part of him he had hidden for far too long. With a nod, he whispered, "Yes, Mistress Victoria, I'm ready."

A knowing smile curved Mistress Victoria's lips as she took a step closer, her latex-clad body inches away from his. The room seemed to crackle with anticipation as their worlds collided, desires intertwining in a dance of dominance and submission.

"In that case, Edward," she whispered, her voice sending shivers down his spine, "let us begin."

And so, within the hallowed walls of the Latex Asylum, Edward's journey into the realm of pleasure, pain, and self-discovery commenced under the guiding hand of Mistress Victoria, the embodiment of dominance and desire.

Chapter 2: Therapy Unleashed

Mistress Victoria exuded an air of dominance as she entered the room, her presence commanding attention. Her long, silky black hair cascaded over her shoulders, contrasting beautifully with her porcelain skin. Her eyes, a piercing shade of emerald green, held a captivating depth, promising both pleasure and pain.

Dressed in a skintight latex nurse uniform, she was a vision of power and sensuality. The glossy material clung to every curve, accentuating her hourglass figure. The uniform consisted of a knee-length dress, featuring a high collar and short, puffed sleeves. The bodice hugged her voluptuous bosom, emphasizing her ample cleavage, while the skirt flared out slightly, showcasing her shapely hips and long, toned legs.

The latex nurse uniform was jet black, providing a striking contrast against her pale skin. It shimmered under the soft glow of the room's dim lighting, its reflective surface hinting at the mysteries it concealed. The dress was cinched at the waist with a wide, glossy black belt, emphasizing her slim middle and adding a touch of elegance to her commanding presence.

Completing her ensemble were thigh-high latex stockings, clinging tightly to her toned thighs, and stiletto heels that accentuated her already impressive height. The heels clicked rhythmically against the floor as she approached Edward, a teasing reminder of her authority.

Edward, his naked body secured to the padded examination table, eagerly awaited the start of his therapy session. His heart raced, a mix of nervousness and anticipation filling his chest. The dimly lit room seemed to pulse with an electric energy as Mistress Victoria circled him, her eyes taking in every inch of his exposed form.

A faint smile played on her lips as she observed Edward's reactions. She could sense his desires, his yearning to surrender himself completely to her control. With a gentle but firm touch, she ran her latex-gloved fingers across his chest, tracing delicate patterns that sent shivers of pleasure down his spine.

"Edward," she purred, her voice laced with a blend of authority and seduction, "we will embark on a journey together, exploring the depths of your desires and unraveling the complexities of your mind."

As Mistress Victoria moved around the table, her latex-clad body brushed against Edward's skin, leaving a trail of goosebumps in its wake. Each contact, deliberate and calculated, heightened his senses, igniting a fire within him that only she could quench.

She paused, leaning in close to his ear, her breath warm against his skin. "You crave my dominance, Edward," she whispered, her voice a velvet caress. "You long to surrender yourself to me, to let go of control and embrace the freedom that comes with submission."

Edward's body trembled in response, his mind consumed by a heady mix of fear and desire. He had never encountered someone who could understand the depths of his needs so effortlessly, who could navigate the intricate pathways of his psyche with such ease.

Mistress Victoria reached for a small tray adorned with an array of gleaming medical instruments. Her latex gloves, snugly fitting her delicate hands, glided effortlessly over the tray's surface as she selected her tools of pleasure and pain.

With a calculated precision, she began her exploration, tracing the contours of Edward's body with various implements. Each touch, each stroke, sent a surge of electricity through his veins. She elicited both pleasure and pain, skillfully dancing along the line that separated the two, pushing Edward further into the depths of his desires.

Time seemed to lose meaning as Mistress Victoria guided Edward through a symphony of sensations. Her touch, soft yet commanding, awakened dormant desires within him, unlocking a world he had only dreamed of. She expertly blended the realms of pleasure and pain, creating a tapestry of sensations that overwhelmed his senses.

As the session neared its end, Mistress Victoria leaned over Edward, her latex-clad form enveloping him in a seductive embrace. She whispered words of encouragement and guidance, urging him to embrace his true desires, to surrender himself fully and without hesitation.

"You are mine, Edward," she murmured, her voice a velvet promise. "In this realm, under my care, you will discover the liberation that comes with surrender. Let go, and together we shall traverse the intoxicating path of pleasure and self-discovery."

With those words hanging in the air, Mistress Victoria pressed her lips gently against Edward's forehead, sealing their unspoken pact. The therapy session had only just begun, and Edward knew that under her skilled guidance, he would be transformed, liberated, and forever changed by the power of Mistress Victoria and her latex-clad dominion.

Chapter 3: A Latex Restriction

Mistress Victoria glided into the room, her presence emanating dominance and allure. Edward's breath hitched as he took in her appearance. The room seemed to shrink, and all that remained was the stunning dominatrix nurse before him.

Her long hair cascaded down her back in waves, framing her porcelain face. Deep, smoky eyes held a knowing glint, their intensity piercing through Edward's soul. A mischievous smile curved her glossy, scarlet lips, hinting at the pleasures she had in store for him.

Mistress Victoria's attire was a masterpiece of latex craftsmanship. The skintight nurse uniform clung to her every curve, accentuating her slender waist and voluptuous hips. The glossy material embraced her body like a second skin, highlighting her powerful presence. The top of the uniform revealed a hint of cleavage, teasing Edward's imagination with the promise of hidden treasures.

The uniform's short, pleated skirt showcased her long, toned legs, encased in thigh-high latex stockings. Each step she took caused a soft, sensuous rustle, adding to the symphony of desire that filled the room. Completing her ensemble were knee-high, high-heeled boots, their shiny black surface mirroring the intensity of her gaze.

As Edward sat bound to the padded examination table, anticipation coursed through his veins. His bare flesh tingled against the coolness of the table's surface, a stark contrast to the warmth that radiated from Mistress

Victoria's presence. The scent of latex filled the air, adding to the intoxicating atmosphere that enveloped them.

Mistress Victoria approached him with measured steps, her movements a dance of seduction and power. Her latex-clad hand grazed his cheek, eliciting a shiver that ran down his spine. "You've been longing for restraint, haven't you, Edward?" she whispered, her voice laced with velvet seduction.

Edward's voice caught in his throat as he nodded, unable to articulate his deepest desires. It was as if Mistress Victoria could read his thoughts, discerning his unspoken fantasies. She reached for a carefully prepared bundle on the nearby table, her latex gloves gliding over the cool surface, each movement deliberate and purposeful.

With a flick of her wrist, Mistress Victoria unfolded a body-hugging latex straitjacket. The glossy material glistened under the room's soft lighting, its inherent allure promising a world of pleasure and surrender. She stepped closer to Edward, allowing him to feel the static charge of her presence.

"Lean back, Edward," she commanded, her voice leaving no room for hesitation. Edward complied, settling against the padded table, his body vulnerable and exposed. Mistress Victoria's nimble fingers worked swiftly, securing the straitjacket around him, the tight embrace of latex binding him with exquisite precision.

Edward's breathing quickened as the latex constricted around his torso, amplifying every sensation. He could feel the pressure of the material against his chest, the seductive friction as Mistress Victoria fastened each strap. His body, now enveloped in the confines of the latex straitjacket, surrendered completely to her control.

Mistress Victoria circled him, her eyes tracing the contours of his restrained form. She caressed his face, her latex-gloved fingers tracing delicate patterns along his jawline. "You're mine now, Edward," she murmured, her voice a potent blend of reassurance and dominance.

With a commanding gesture, Mistress Victoria beckoned Edward to look into her eyes. "Relax, my dear," she coaxed, her voice a seductive melody. "Let go of your worries and surrender to the pleasure I will bestow upon you."

As Edward's body settled into the tight embrace of the latex straitjacket, Mistress Victoria leaned in, her lips barely grazing his earlobe. "I control your pleasure, your pain, and everything in between," she whispered, the words sending a surge of electricity through Edward's veins.

The session had only just begun, and already, Edward could feel the boundaries of his desires expanding. In the confines of the Latex Asylum, under the guidance of Mistress Victoria, he would embark on a journey of self-discovery and liberation. Bound in latex, his body restricted yet alive with anticipation, Edward surrendered himself to the whims and desires of the dominant nurse who held his heart and mind captive.

Chapter 4: The Electrotherapy Experiment

Mistress Victoria's eyes glimmered with a mix of intrigue and anticipation as she contemplated the potential of electrotherapy. It was a realm of exploration she had long yearned to delve into, a world where pain and pleasure danced on the electrified edge. She had prepared her laboratory meticulously, the sterile space now tingling with an undercurrent of excitement.

Edward, her devoted patient, awaited her presence with bated breath. His heart pounded against his chest, a rhythm that mirrored the pulsating currents that would soon course through his body. Dressed in a tailored black suit, he exuded an air of vulnerability that only fueled Mistress Victoria's desire to guide him through this electrifying experiment.

Mistress Victoria's appearance was a testament to her dominion over the realm of latex. Her cascading chestnut locks tumbled down her back in wild waves, contrasting against the porcelain smoothness of her complexion. Her piercing blue eyes, framed by lashes that flirted with temptation, seemed to hold a mysterious secret within their depths.

Clad in a skintight, jet-black latex nurse uniform, every curve and contour of her body was accentuated with meticulous precision. The fabric hugged her form like a second skin, whispering of seduction and power. The low-cut neckline revealed a tantalizing glimpse of her ample cleavage, a teasing invitation to explore the depths of her dominance.

Gloved hands, encased in latex that matched the inky hue of her uniform, appeared both delicate and commanding. They moved with a grace born from a profound understanding of her patients' desires and limitations. On this occasion, she adorned her gloves with electrically conductive pads, their presence an indication of the electrifying journey about to unfold.

Mistress Victoria led Edward into the laboratory, its atmosphere charged with anticipation. The air seemed to crackle with energy, mirroring the magnetic pull that drew them together. The room was bathed in dim lighting, the shadows adding an ethereal quality to their surroundings. Machinery hummed softly, a symphony of anticipation that resonated within both of them.

Edward's gaze locked onto Mistress Victoria, his eyes fixated on her every movement. Her confidence radiated like an aura, enveloping him in a sense of trust and submission. He knew he was in capable hands, guided by a woman who understood the delicate balance of pleasure and pain.

As he settled into the metal chair, its cold touch sending a shiver up his spine, Edward's anticipation mingled with a slight trepidation. He had surrendered himself to Mistress Victoria's care, giving her control over his pleasure and pain. It was a heady mix of vulnerability and exhilaration, a potent elixir that fueled his desires.

Mistress Victoria's gloved hands glided over the smooth surface of the machinery, her touch both purposeful and seductive. She connected the wires and adjusted the settings with a deft precision, ensuring that every jolt of electricity would be delivered with calculated intensity.

Turning to face Edward, Mistress Victoria's gaze bore into his soul, as if searching for any lingering doubts or hesitations. "Edward," she purred, her voice a melodic blend of authority and intimacy, "are you ready to surrender to the electrifying sensations that await you?"

Edward's voice quivered slightly as he replied, "Yes, Mistress Victoria. I trust you completely."

A smile tugged at the corners of her perfectly sculpted lips. "Good," she whispered, her breath warm against his skin. "Prepare yourself, Edward, for a journey that will awaken your senses and transcend the boundaries of pleasure."

With a flick of her gloved finger, Mistress Victoria activated the machine, and a low hum filled the room. The currents began to flow, a gentle caress that gradually intensified, sending waves of anticipation rippling through Edward's body. As the electricity coursed through him, his senses became heightened, each touch, each sensation magnified.

Mistress Victoria moved with purpose, skillfully maneuvering the pads along Edward's body, ensuring that every nerve was ignited with desire. Her touch alternated between sweet torment and exquisite release, her gloved hands tracing a path of electrifying pleasure over his exposed skin.

Edward surrendered to the sensations, his body a conduit for the power that Mistress Victoria wielded.

Each surge of electricity became an intoxicating dance between pain and pleasure, pushing him to the edge and then gently reeling him back.

As the experiment reached its climax, Mistress Victoria watched Edward with a mix of satisfaction and affection. She had guided him through this journey of electrifying liberation, tapping into the depths of his desires and unlocking a world of pleasure that had been waiting to be unleashed.

With the flick of a switch, Mistress Victoria deactivated the machine, the currents dissipating into the air. She released Edward from the chair, his body trembling with the aftermath of the electrifying encounter. As he stood before her, a newfound sense of freedom emanated from him, his soul ignited by the power of their connection.

Mistress Victoria approached Edward, her eyes sparkling with an understanding born from their shared journey. She cupped his face in her gloved hands, her touch both tender and possessive. "You've done wonderfully, Edward," she murmured, her voice a velvet caress against his ear. "Embrace the electricity that courses through your veins, for it is a reminder of the liberation found in surrender."

As Edward gazed into Mistress Victoria's eyes, he knew that this electrifying experiment had forever transformed him. He had not only discovered the power of electrotherapy but had also found solace and fulfillment in the capable hands of his Latex Asylum mistress.

Chapter 5: The Power of Sensory Deprivation

The room was cloaked in an air of mystery, its dim lighting casting seductive shadows against the glossy latex walls. Mistress Victoria led Edward, his senses already heightened in anticipation, into the heart of this intimate sanctum. The heavy scent of latex engulfed him, intoxicating his every breath.

Dressed in a provocative latex nurse outfit, Mistress Victoria exuded an aura of dominance and sensuality. Her form-fitting uniform embraced her curves, accentuating her lithe frame. Jet-black hair cascaded down her back, contrasting beautifully against her porcelain skin. Her piercing green eyes held a blend of command and compassion, captivating Edward with their hypnotic allure.

Her attire was a masterpiece of latex craftsmanship. The nurse's cap sat perched on her head, adorned with a red cross, a symbol of both her authority and the tantalizing pleasures she promised. The neckline of her uniform plunged seductively, exposing a hint of cleavage that tantalized Edward's imagination. The tight, short sleeves hugged her arms, highlighting their toned elegance. The skirt clung to her hips, flaring out slightly, showcasing her shapely legs.

As they reached the heart of the room, Mistress Victoria guided Edward to a padded, latex-covered bed, its surface cool and inviting. The atmosphere was charged with anticipation, the weight of their desires hanging heavy in the air.

"Edward," Mistress Victoria's voice cooed, a velvety smoothness that sent shivers down his spine. "Today, we shall explore the power of sensory deprivation. Are you ready to surrender yourself completely?"

Edward nodded, his heart pounding in his chest. He yearned to submit to her, to be enveloped in a world where only her commands mattered. As he disrobed, his body exposed to her piercing gaze, he felt vulnerable yet liberated, the latex-clad Mistress Victoria becoming the sole focus of his attention.

From a drawer nearby, Mistress Victoria retrieved a black latex hood. Its glossy surface gleamed under the soft illumination of the room. The inside was lined with a soft, cushioned material, designed to ensure both comfort and restriction.

She approached Edward, the latex gloves on her hands sliding smoothly against his bare skin. With practiced precision, she positioned the hood, its tight embrace molding to the contours of his face. As the latex sealed around his eyes, nose, and mouth, his world was plunged into darkness, silence, and a heightened awareness of every sensation.

Edward's breathing quickened, the sound amplified in the confined darkness of the hood. He could feel the weight of Mistress Victoria's presence, her proximity electrifying his senses. Her fingers gently traced patterns along the latex covering his cheeks, her touch igniting a flicker of desire within him.

"Edward," her voice whispered, her words sending shivers through his body. "In this darkness, you shall find liberation. Your senses are stripped bare, leaving you vulnerable to my every touch, my every command. Trust in me, and surrender yourself to the power of this moment."

The world outside the hood melted away, leaving only the realm of touch, sound, and imagination. Mistress Victoria's voice became his guiding light, her instructions painting vivid scenes in his mind's eye. Every whisper, every breath against his ear, transported him deeper into the realm of submission and ecstasy.

The sensation of Mistress Victoria's latex-clad hands against his body became intensified, each caress sending waves of pleasure coursing through him. He felt her exploring him, teasing him, awakening every inch of his flesh. She alternated between gentle strokes and firm grips, pushing him to the edge of desire, only to withdraw and leave him yearning for more.

Time lost its meaning in the darkness of the hood. Edward's focus narrowed solely on the sensations bestowed upon him, the symphony of latex and desire intertwining in a dance of pleasure and submission. Mistress Victoria's mastery was evident in every touch, every command that guided him towards a heightened state of bliss.

As the session neared its conclusion, Mistress Victoria removed the hood with a gentle tug, revealing Edward's face to the world once more. The room came back into focus, the subdued lighting caressing his eyes.

Edward's body felt alive, pulsating with the echoes of his encounter with sensory deprivation. He gazed at Mistress Victoria, gratitude and reverence reflected in his eyes. Through the power of latex and her expert touch, she had unveiled a deeper realm of pleasure within him, igniting a fire that would forever burn in his soul.

Mistress Victoria smiled, a knowing glint in her eyes. "You have experienced the power of surrender, Edward. Embrace it, cherish it. Our journey has only just begun."

And in that moment, Edward knew that his life would forever be entwined with the beguiling dominatrix nurse who had awakened his desires and liberated his spirit.

Chapter 6: Liberation Through Surrender

As the journey of Edward's therapy at the Latex Asylum neared its climax, Mistress Victoria sensed that he was on the precipice of a transformative breakthrough. She meticulously planned a session that would push the boundaries of his submission and set him free from the chains of societal expectations.

The door to the specially prepared chamber swung open, revealing a dimly lit room adorned with mirrors and soft ambient lighting. Edward's breath caught in his throat as he took in the scene before him. At the center of the room stood Mistress Victoria, radiating an aura of dominance and sensuality that was impossible to ignore.

Her appearance had undergone a remarkable transformation. Her cascading dark locks were swept up into an intricate braided updo, accentuating the elegant lines of her face. Her eyes, smoldering with a mix of power and compassion, held a spark of mischief that thrilled Edward to his core. Her lips, painted a deep shade of crimson, curled into a sly smile as she observed his reaction.

Mistress Victoria's attire was a masterpiece of latex artistry. She wore a form-fitting black latex corset that accentuated her hourglass figure, molding to every curve and contour of her body. The corset was embellished with intricate lacing that crisscrossed from top to bottom, symbolizing the intertwining of dominance and submission. Her ample bosom was showcased with a tantalizing plunge, leaving just enough to the imagination. The latex material clung to her like a second skin, highlighting the lustrous shine that reflected the surrounding light.

Below her waist, she wore a matching black latex skirt that hugged her hips, flaring out slightly to emphasize her feminine allure. The skirt grazed her thighs, revealing just a hint of the silky stockings that encased her legs. Every movement she made created a symphony of whispers, the sound of latex gliding against latex, amplifying the electrifying tension in the room.

Adorning her feet were sky-high stiletto heels, the glossy black latex material extending upward to form intricate straps that wrapped around her ankles. They accentuated her graceful posture, elevating her dominance to even greater heights. With each step she took, the sound of her heels echoed throughout the chamber, a rhythmic symphony that resonated in Edward's soul.

As Edward's eyes traveled upward, he noticed a small, delicate pendant nestled in the hollow of her collarbone. The pendant, a symbol of their journey together, depicted a fusion of a heart and a latex corset, a tangible reminder of their connection and the transformation he had undergone under her guidance.

Mistress Victoria approached Edward, her movements fluid and purposeful. Her gloved hand reached out, inviting him to join her in this final act of liberation. With a mixture of anticipation and trepidation, he stepped forward, his eyes locked with hers.

"I have prepared something special for you, Edward," she whispered, her voice low and velvety, enveloping him like a warm embrace. "Today, we will embrace the full power of surrender, the merging of your desires with mine."

He nodded, his heart pounding in his chest, as Mistress Victoria led him to a plush, cushioned bench at the center of the room. The bench, upholstered in black leather, beckoned him to lie down, offering himself completely to her.

As he settled onto the bench, Mistress Victoria began the ritual of his surrender. She secured his wrists and ankles with soft, supple leather restraints, ensuring his safety while creating a sense of vulnerability that would pave the way for his ultimate liberation. Each strap was tightened with just enough tension to remind him of his submission, the juxtaposition of pleasure and restraint merging into a potent cocktail of sensations.

Once Edward was fully restrained, Mistress Victoria stood back, her eyes tracing the contours of his body with a hunger that both excited and comforted him. The room seemed to pulse with anticipation as she reached for a nearby table, upon which a selection of latex implements awaited.

With a deliberate grace, Mistress Victoria chose a latex flogger, its sleek and supple strands promising both pleasure and pain. As she circled around him, her eyes locked onto his, their connection unbreakable, she drew the flogger across his skin, each caress igniting a fire within him.

The first strike landed with a resounding thud, the impact rippling through his body. The sensation was both thrilling and grounding, the pain awakening a dormant part of his soul. With each subsequent strike, Mistress Victoria expertly controlled the intensity, guiding him on a journey of catharsis.

As the flogger danced across his body, a symphony of sensation played out within him. The sharp sting of the impact melded with the soft caress of latex against his sensitized skin, creating a dance of pleasure and pain that pushed him to the edge of his limits.

With each strike, Mistress Victoria whispered words of encouragement and guidance, her voice a soothing balm to his soul. Her presence was a beacon of strength and understanding, allowing him to surrender completely to the waves of emotion crashing over him.

As the session progressed, Mistress Victoria knew that Edward was on the brink of his ultimate liberation. She discarded the flogger and, with a slow, deliberate movement, she peeled off her latex gloves, exposing her bare hands. Her touch against his reddened skin was electrifying, sending shivers down his spine.

Her touch became a caress, her hands mapping the contours of his body with an intimate knowledge that left him breathless. As she pressed against his back, her body molded to his, a physical representation of their connection and the merging of their desires.

In that moment of profound vulnerability, Edward understood the true power of surrender. The boundaries that had once confined him were shattered, replaced by a newfound freedom and acceptance of his desires. Mistress Victoria had guided him to this transformative state, unlocking a part of him that yearned to be seen, accepted, and embraced.

With a final, gentle stroke, Mistress Victoria leaned in close, her lips brushing against his ear. "You have surrendered, Edward," she whispered, her voice a mixture of triumph and tenderness. "You are free to embrace your desires, your true self."

Tears welled in Edward's eyes as he absorbed her words, his heart overflowing with gratitude and a sense of rebirth. In the arms of Mistress Victoria, he had found solace, acceptance, and the courage to embrace his deepest longings.

Together, they basked in the afterglow of his liberation, the echoes of their journey reverberating through the chamber. In that moment, Edward realized that his time at the Latex Asylum had not only transformed him but had bound him to Mistress Victoria in a way that transcended the physical.

As they savored the stillness, Mistress Victoria gently released his restraints, setting him free from their physical confines. But their connection remained unbreakable, a testament to the profound impact she had on his life.

Edward, now liberated and unburdened, stood alongside Mistress Victoria, ready to face a future unbound by the chains of societal expectations. The journey had been arduous, but through the power of surrender, they had both found solace, acceptance, and love in the most unexpected of places.

Latex Emergency Response

Chapter 1: The Call of Duty

The shrill sound of the emergency alarm sliced through the stillness of Nurse Helena's bedroom, abruptly interrupting her dreams. In an instant, her vibrant blue eyes fluttered open, a mix of excitement and determination illuminating her gaze. She was a woman who thrived in the face of chaos, her slender frame exuding an air of confidence that matched her profession.

Throwing aside the silken sheets, Helena rose from her bed, her lithe form swathed in nothing but a sheer lace robe. Her long, dark locks cascaded in loose waves down her back, framing a face that boasted flawless porcelain skin, high cheekbones, and a pair of sensual lips that hinted at a hint of mischief. But it was her eyes that held the allure, captivating orbs that seemed to hold a secret, a desire yet to be fulfilled.

With each deliberate step, Helena glided across her room, moving with a grace that was both enticing and hypnotic. Her wardrobe, a meticulously organized collection of latex attire, beckoned her with promise and purpose. She was a woman who embraced her passions unapologetically, unafraid to explore the depths of her desires.

As the latex garments hung before her, each piece a second skin that clung to her every curve, Helena pondered her choice for the day. Today, she opted for a form-fitting latex nurse uniform, the glossy black fabric hugging her body like a lover's embrace. The ensemble featured a low-cut neckline that accentuated her ample bosom, teasingly leaving just enough to the imagination. The short, flared skirt revealed her shapely legs, encased in thigh-high latex stockings that further accentuated her sensual appeal.

With practiced ease, Helena slipped into the latex uniform, the material adhering to her like a second skin. She reveled in the sensation—the smoothness, the tightness—it was as if the latex understood her desires and catered to them, amplifying her confidence and dominance.

Completing her ensemble, she fastened the glossy black gloves that reached her elbows, relishing in the control they afforded her. The final touch was a pair of towering stiletto heels, their sleek design elevating her stature and commanding attention.

Standing before the full-length mirror, Helena admired her reflection. The latex-clad nurse stared back at her, a woman who was both a symbol of authority and an embodiment of untamed sensuality. The latex accentuated her every contour, molding itself to her body as if it were an extension of her own skin. It was a visual representation of her power, an armor that shielded her vulnerability while simultaneously inviting others to explore the depths of their desires.

As the emergency alarm continued to blare, Helena's mind snapped back to the present. With one final adjustment of her latex attire, she strode purposefully out of her bedroom, ready to face the challenges that awaited her. She was a dominatrix nurse, a woman who held the dual role of healer and seductress, and the call of duty beckoned her with a magnetic pull.

Through the hospital corridors she walked, her heels clicking in rhythm with her heartbeat. The whispers and glances that followed her were evidence of the captivating aura she exuded—a combination of authority and allure that left those around her spellbound.

As she entered the bustling emergency room, Helena's eyes scanned the room, seeking out her team members. The Latex Emergency Response team was a force to be reckoned with, each member sharing her passion for both medical expertise and the intoxicating allure of latex. Together, they would face the most daunting medical situations with a unique blend of professionalism and erotic energy.

As the chaos of the emergency room swirled around her, Helena stood at the epicenter, ready to command the battlefield. Her latex uniform, gleaming under the harsh fluorescent lights, became a symbol of both her role as a nurse and her dominance as a woman unafraid to explore her deepest desires.

In that moment, Nurse Helena embraced her dual nature—a healer and a seductress. With every breath she took, she reveled in the power that her latex-clad persona granted her—the power to heal, the power to dominate, and the power to fulfill the fantasies that lay dormant within her patients and herself.

The call of duty had summoned her, and she would answer it with unwavering determination, her latex-clad allure captivating all those who dared to cross her path.

Chapter 2: Tangled Desires

Helena stood amidst the wreckage, her heart pounding in sync with the blaring sirens that echoed through the air. With her latex-clad team by her side, she exuded an aura of confidence and control. Her eyes darted across the chaotic scene, assessing the situation, but something caught her attention—a pair of intense green eyes locked onto hers.

Ethan, a rugged firefighter with tousled dark hair and a chiseled jawline, stood tall amidst the chaos. His uniform, smudged with dirt and soot, clung to his muscular frame. He exuded a raw masculinity that sent shivers down Helena's spine. She found herself irresistibly drawn to him, their connection burning with an intensity that defied the surrounding chaos.

Helena's own appearance matched her confident nature. Her lustrous chestnut locks cascaded in loose waves around her shoulders, framing a face adorned with deep, penetrating eyes that held a hint of mystery. Her porcelain skin seemed to glow against the glossy black latex uniform that hugged every curve of her voluptuous figure. The sleek material clung to her like a second skin, accentuating her ample bosom, narrow waist, and perfectly sculpted hips. A crimson cross emblem adorned the left side of her uniform, signifying her role as a dominatrix nurse.

As the emergency crews worked tirelessly to secure the accident scene, Helena found herself unable to tear her gaze away from Ethan. His commanding presence and rugged charm were a potent combination that stirred a longing within her she had not felt in a long time. The adrenaline-fueled atmosphere heightened their desire, creating an electric connection that seemed to crackle in the air.

Their eyes met again, and Helena couldn't resist the allure any longer. She motioned for Ethan to join her, leading him to a quieter corner away from prying eyes. Surrounded by the remnants of twisted metal and the faint smell of smoke, they found solace in their shared passion for latex and the undeniable chemistry that simmered between them.

Ethan's calloused hands traced the contours of Helena's latex-clad body, his touch sending waves of pleasure through her. The glossy material heightened every sensation, making her skin tingle with delight. Helena reveled in the power dynamics that unfolded between them—a dominant nurse surrendering control to a rugged firefighter.

The uniform became their conduit for desire, each inch of latex a tactile reminder of their shared kink. The sound of latex stretching and caressing skin filled the air, mingling with their breathless moans and whispered commands. Helena, with her commanding presence, took the lead, guiding Ethan into a world of pleasure that danced on the edge of pain.

Their passion intensified with each moment, their bodies becoming entwined like flames licking at the darkness. The blend of dominance and submission swirled in the air, as Ethan willingly surrendered to Helena's expert touch. Her latex-clad form pressed against his, igniting a fire within him that burned hotter than any flame he had ever encountered.

Time stood still in that secluded corner, as Helena and Ethan explored the depths of their desires. Their encounter was more than physical—it was an exploration of trust, vulnerability, and a shared understanding of the power that lay within their chosen attire.

As the accident scene slowly regained order, Helena and Ethan reluctantly emerged from their hidden sanctuary. Their connection, however, remained etched deep within their souls, promising more tantalizing encounters to come. In that moment, they realized that their tangled desires were far from being extinguished—they had only just begun to explore the intoxicating realm of latex and the fiery passion that burned between them.

Chapter 3: A Healing Touch

Nurse Helena stood in the dimly lit corridor, her pulse quickening as she watched Ethan, the rugged firefighter, approach her. His smoldering gaze matched the intensity of the emergency room's atmosphere. With every step he took, the desire between them grew, igniting a longing that could no longer be denied.

Helena was a striking woman in her late twenties, blessed with cascading chestnut curls that framed her porcelain face. Her sapphire eyes held a mischievous glimmer, hinting at the hidden depths of her desires. Standing at an average height, her toned figure exuded both strength and sensuality, drawing attention wherever she went.

But it was her attire that truly set Helena apart. She adorned her body with an array of latex garments that clung to her curves like a second skin. Her uniform, a glossy black ensemble, consisted of a form-fitting latex blouse that accentuated her ample bosom, paired with a high-waisted pencil skirt that showcased her slender waist and shapely hips. The skirt ended just above her knees, revealing her toned legs, encased in sheer black stockings.

Completing her ensemble were knee-high stiletto boots, their shiny latex material enhancing her already commanding presence. Helena embraced the allure of latex not only for its provocative aesthetic but also for the way it amplified her confidence, empowering her as she navigated her professional and personal desires.

As the chaos of the emergency room unfolded, Helena and Ethan found solace in each other's company. It was during a brief respite that their eyes met, the magnetic pull between them almost tangible. Unspoken words filled the air, heavy with anticipation and longing.

Ethan, his broad shoulders encased in firefighter gear, approached Helena, his eyes filled with a mixture of admiration and desire. "You're incredible," he murmured, his voice laced with awe.

Helena's lips curved into a seductive smile as she assessed him, her fingers gently brushing against his strong forearm. "And you, Ethan, are a hero," she replied, her voice a soft purr. "We both know the power of the uniform."

Their conversation became a dance of innuendos and stolen glances, the tension escalating with each passing moment. The allure of their latex-clad bodies, the embodiment of dominance and submission, became impossible to resist. With an unspoken agreement, they sought a secluded corner of the hospital, away from prying eyes.

In a room filled with latex-covered equipment, their desires intertwined, their bodies becoming a symphony of pleasure and passion. Helena reveled in the feel of the smooth latex against her skin as Ethan explored her curves with reverent hands. The material accentuated every touch, every caress, heightening their connection and intensifying their pleasure.

Time stood still as their bodies merged, the air heavy with the heady scent of desire. Helena's body arched beneath Ethan's touch, her latex-covered form yielding to his every command. Their mutual hunger for control and surrender melded seamlessly, pushing them both to the brink of ecstasy.

As their encounter reached its climax, Helena's mind and body reveled in the liberation that latex provided. It was more than a material; it was an extension of herself, a conduit for her deepest desires. In that moment of shared vulnerability and intimate connection, Helena and Ethan experienced a new level of pleasure, where latex and passion intertwined in a dance of dominance and submission.

Breathless and sated, they lay entwined on a latex-covered examination table, basking in the aftermath of their encounter. Their eyes locked, understanding passing between them, as they knew their journey was far from over. The allure of latex had only ignited their appetite for exploration, and they were both eager to discover where their desires would lead them next.

With each encounter, Nurse Helena embraced the liberating power of latex, transforming it into a vessel for her fantasies, a tangible expression of her deepest longings. As her story unfolded, the boundaries between her professional duties and her insatiable appetite blurred, and the world of dominance and submission merged seamlessly with the provocative embrace of latex.

Chapter 4: Intensive Care

Nurse Helena had always possessed an air of confidence, and her striking appearance only added to her allure. With long, flowing chestnut locks cascading down her shoulders and captivating hazel eyes that held a mischievous spark, she exuded a magnetic presence that captivated both patients and colleagues alike. Her petite yet curvaceous figure was accentuated by her form-fitting latex uniform, meticulously tailored to hug every enticing curve.

As she prepared to enter the intensive care unit, Helena meticulously adjusted her attire, ensuring that every inch of her latex outfit was flawlessly in place. The glossy material clung to her like a second skin, leaving little to the imagination. The top, with its plunging neckline, showcased a tantalizing hint of her ample cleavage, while the skin-tight pencil skirt emphasized the sway of her hips and the gentle curve of her derrière.

Her outfit was completed with long latex gloves that stretched up to her elbows, their sheen adding a touch of elegance and dominance to her overall appearance. The scent of latex enveloped her, heightening her senses and empowering her with a newfound confidence. Helena reveled in the way her attire transformed her from a nurse into a dominatrix, ready to navigate the complexities of the medical world while indulging in her deepest desires.

Inside the intensive care unit, the air was thick with tension. The relentless beep of monitors and hushed whispers of doctors created a symphony of urgency.

Helena's attention, however, was immediately drawn to a patient named Rachel. Pale and vulnerable, Rachel lay amidst a sea of medical equipment, her soft brown eyes searching for solace.

Approaching Rachel's bedside, Helena exuded an air of authority and compassion. She was a master at the delicate dance of dominance and care, knowing precisely when to assert her power and when to offer a gentle touch. With a confident smile, she introduced herself, her latex-gloved hand lightly brushing against Rachel's trembling fingers.

"Hello, Rachel," Helena purred, her voice laced with a subtle undertone of command. "I'm Nurse Helena. I'm here to take care of you."

Rachel's gaze flickered between Helena's eyes and the tantalizing sight of latex hugging her form. A mixture of curiosity and desire swirled within her, as if she had been drawn into a seductive web woven by the nurse's aura. There was something irresistible about Helena's presence—a magnetic force that beckoned Rachel to surrender.

As the days turned into nights, Helena devoted herself to Rachel's care. She administered medications with a practiced precision, her latex-clad hands gliding effortlessly over Rachel's delicate skin. The touch of latex against bare flesh created a sensual friction that stirred desires within both women, awakening dormant cravings they had long suppressed.

With each encounter, the bond between nurse and patient deepened. Helena sensed Rachel's unspoken yearning, her hidden longing for surrender. And as a skilled dominatrix, she knew how to awaken and explore those desires.

One night, under the soft glow of the dimmed hospital lights, Helena entered Rachel's room, her latex attire shimmering like liquid midnight. Rachel's breath hitched as she watched the nurse approach, her eyes filled with a mix of trepidation and longing.

Helena locked the door, creating an intimate space where their desires could finally be unleashed. She moved with a graceful confidence, her latex-clad body exuding power and sensuality. Her gloved hand gently caressed Rachel's cheek, the coolness of the latex contrasting with the warmth of their connection.

"I'm here to heal more than just your body, Rachel," Helena whispered, her voice a seductive melody. "I want to awaken the depths of your desires, to guide you to a place where surrender becomes your ultimate liberation."

Rachel's heart raced as Helena's words washed over her, the prospect of surrender and exploration both exhilarating and terrifying. With a single nod, she granted Helena permission to delve into the depths of her being, to traverse the uncharted territories of her desires.

And so, within the confines of the hospital room, nurse and patient delved into a realm where latex became a conduit for pleasure and submission. Boundaries blurred as Helena expertly guided Rachel through a journey of dominance and surrender, using the aesthetics and power dynamics of latex to explore the vast possibilities of their connection.

As the night unfolded, moans of pleasure and whispered commands filled the room. Helena reveled in the intoxicating power she held over Rachel, and Rachel, in turn, discovered liberation in her surrender. The encounter merged the realms of medical care and BDSM, as Helena administered not only physical healing but also unleashed the transformative power of submission and dominance.

As the night waned and the intensity of their encounter subsided, Helena remained by Rachel's side, her touch a gentle reassurance that their connection extended beyond the boundaries of latex and desire. In that intimate space, the dominatrix nurse had healed more than just Rachel's body; she had awakened a profound sense of liberation and self-discovery.

And in the midst of their shared desires and unspoken vulnerabilities, Nurse Helena found solace, knowing that within the fusion of latex and passion, she had unraveled the intricate tapestry of human connection and unleashed the transformative power of healing.

Chapter 5: The Late-Night Encounter

The moon hung high in the night sky, casting an ethereal glow upon the rooftop of the hospital. Nurse Helena's steps were hushed as she made her way to the secluded spot, her heart pounding in anticipation. Dressed in a form-fitting latex uniform, her every movement accentuated by the sleek, glossy material, she exuded an aura of commanding allure.

Helena was a woman of striking beauty, with cascading raven hair that fell in gentle waves around her face, framing piercing emerald eyes that held a glimmer of mischief. Her lips, painted a deep crimson, hinted at a sensuality that stirred something primal within those who dared to meet her gaze. Her porcelain skin was flawless, save for a small tattoo—a delicate black rose—adorned just above her left collarbone, a hidden symbol of her inner desires.

Tonight, Helena had chosen a latex ensemble that hugged her curves in all the right places. The glossy black material clung to her like a second skin, accentuating her slender waist and ample bosom. The high collar of her uniform added an air of authority, while the silver accents shimmered under the moonlight, beckoning to be explored.

As she reached the rooftop, Helena's eyes scanned the dark expanse, seeking the one person who had been watching her from afar. Dr. Gabriel, a man with a reputation for his darkly handsome features and commanding presence, stood near the edge, his gaze fixed on her approach. His neatly trimmed beard emphasized the chiseled contours of his face, adding an air of rugged allure to his already captivating charm.

His attire mirrored Helena's predilection for latex. Draped in a form-fitting black latex suit, he appeared as a commanding figure, exuding an aura of dominance that sent shivers down Helena's spine. The subtle gleam of silver accents adorned his outfit, matching her own, as if they were destined to be intertwined.

As they stood mere feet apart, their eyes locked in an unspoken understanding, a charged silence enveloped them. It was a moment suspended in time, where desire and anticipation hung in the air, palpable and intoxicating.

"Helena," Dr. Gabriel's voice rumbled, the deep timbre sending a delightful shiver down her spine. "I've been watching you from afar, drawn to your beauty, your confidence, and your love for latex."

A blush warmed Helena's cheeks as she listened to his words, her heart racing with a mixture of excitement and trepidation. The rooftop seemed to shrink around them, leaving only their magnetic connection.

Dr. Gabriel closed the distance between them, his hand gently caressing her cheek, the touch sending an electric current through her veins. "Let us explore our desires, Helena," he whispered, his voice heavy with a promise that ignited a fire deep within her.

Without hesitation, Helena surrendered herself to the moment, to the electricity that crackled in the air between them. Their bodies melded together, their latex-clad forms becoming one as they indulged in their shared passion.

Under the moon's watchful eye, they danced a tantalizing tango of dominance and submission, each movement a carefully choreographed expression of their desires. Their hands roamed over slick latex, tracing the contours of one another's bodies, the glossy material amplifying the intensity of their touch.

As their encounter unfolded, the rooftop became their own private sanctuary—a world where latex and desire merged in a symphony of pleasure. Their shared exploration was a delicate balance of power and surrender, a dance of trust and vulnerability that intertwined their souls.

Hours melted away, and as dawn painted the sky with streaks of golden light, Helena and Dr. Gabriel found solace in each other's arms, their bodies glistening with a sheen of perspiration. They lay entwined, a tableau of contentment, knowing that their journey had only just begun.

In that moment, Helena realized that latex was not merely an outer expression of her desires; it was a conduit for the depths of her passion. And with Dr. Gabriel by her side, she knew that their encounters would continue to explore the intricate layers of dominance and submission, all wrapped in the tantalizing embrace of latex.

Together, they were a force to be reckoned with—an intoxicating blend of power, desire, and the seductive allure of latex.

Chapter 6: Unveiling Desires

Nurse Helena stood at the helm of the Latex Emergency Response team, her commanding presence radiating through the room. Her dark tresses cascaded down her back, contrasting against her porcelain skin. With mesmerizing hazel eyes that held a hint of mischief, she had an aura that drew people in, captivating them with a single glance. Her figure was statuesque, accentuated by the skin-tight, glossy black latex uniform she wore, clinging to every curve and leaving little to the imagination. The uniform accentuated her ample bosom, cinched at the waist, and flared out at the hips, revealing the alluring contours of her body.

On this particular night, Helena's attire was heightened to reflect her desires. Her uniform was adorned with intricate lace-up details, adding a touch of elegance to the already provocative ensemble. The long latex gloves reached her elbows, accentuating her slender arms. Her legs were encased in thigh-high latex stockings, held up by garters that peeked out enticingly from beneath her uniform. Completing her ensemble were knee-high, stiletto-heeled boots, accentuating her confident stride and giving her an air of dominance.

Helena had always been aware of her dominant nature, finding solace and excitement in the power exchange that came with it. Alicia, her team member, had caught her attention from the beginning. Alicia's shy demeanor and submissive tendencies ignited a fire within Helena, and she had been observing her from a distance, waiting for the perfect opportunity to explore their shared desires.

As the hazardous chemical spill unfolded, Helena found herself working closely with Alicia. The intensity of the situation heightened their emotions, and Helena sensed Alicia's unspoken yearning. It was in the midst of the chaos that Helena took the lead, subtly asserting her dominance over Alicia, guiding her with a firm yet caring touch.

They retreated to a small, dimly lit room, away from prying eyes. The flickering light from a single candle cast an ethereal glow over their latex-clad bodies. Helena moved with grace, her latex creaking softly with each step. She circled Alicia, her fingertips tracing patterns on Alicia's exposed skin, creating a symphony of sensations.

Alicia's eyes were a mixture of apprehension and anticipation as she submitted to Helena's will. She wore a latex corset that cinched her waist, accentuating her curves. The corset was adorned with delicate lace, teasingly exposing her cleavage. Her matching latex panties hugged her hips, emphasizing her vulnerability. The anticipation in the room was palpable as Helena slowly removed her gloves, exposing her bare hands. With a gentle yet firm grip, she guided Alicia to a bondage bench, carefully securing her wrists and ankles, leaving her exposed and at Helena's mercy.

Helena's voice was a low, sultry purr as she whispered commands, guiding Alicia into a state of blissful surrender. She reveled in the power she held, knowing that Alicia's pleasure was in her hands. Using a variety of latex implements, Helena tantalized Alicia's senses, exploring the fine line between pleasure and pain. Each touch, each stroke, elicited a response, fueling the desire that crackled between them.

Their encounter was a dance of dominance and submission, a symphony of latex-clad bodies intertwining in a beautiful expression of their desires. Time seemed to lose its hold as they delved deeper into the realm of their shared fantasies, pushing boundaries and exploring the depths of their connection.

As the session reached its climax, Helena untied Alicia, cradling her in her arms, their latex-covered bodies pressed against each other. The air crackled with a newfound understanding and a bond forged through trust and exploration.

In that moment, as they lay entwined on the soft latex-covered bed, Helena's heart swelled with a sense of fulfillment. She had uncovered Alicia's desires, bringing them to light and providing a safe space for their expression. And in doing so, she had discovered her own liberation, finding solace in the embrace of her dominant nature.

As the room fell into a tranquil stillness, Helena and Alicia savored the afterglow, their latex uniforms clinging to their satisfied bodies. The journey of their desires had only just begun, and together, they would continue to explore the captivating world of dominance and submission, all wrapped in the seductive embrace of latex.

The Latex Research Facility

Chapter 1: The Mysterious Facility

Dr. Suzie Sinclair, a brilliant and audacious scientist, possessed an alluring mix of intelligence and sensual confidence. Her striking features included piercing green eyes that sparkled with a mischievous glint and cascades of fiery auburn hair that framed her porcelain face. Standing at an average height, her toned figure boasted gentle curves that were accentuated by her favorite ensembles.

When it came to fashion, Dr. Sinclair had a penchant for indulging her latex fetish. Her wardrobe was a carefully curated collection of provocative latex outfits that hugged her body like a second skin. From her form-fitting latex lab coat that accentuated her every curve to her thigh-high latex boots that exuded both power and allure, she embodied a seductive blend of scientific prowess and eroticism.

As Dr. Sinclair arrived at the entrance of the mysterious research facility, she couldn't help but feel a sense of exhilaration coursing through her veins. The building stood as a testament to the enigmatic nature of the experiments conducted within. Its sleek exterior, composed of reflective glass panels, seemed to mirror the secrets that lay within its walls.

Taking a deep breath, Dr. Sinclair adjusted her latex gloves and confidently pushed open the heavy metal doors. A hush fell over her as the imposing entrance swung open, revealing a corridor bathed in sterile white light. The air seemed charged with a unique energy, a palpable anticipation that set her heart racing.

Her footsteps echoed as she ventured further into the facility, her boots emitting a soft, seductive squeak against the polished floors. She navigated the corridors with an air of purpose, her gaze fixated on each laboratory door she passed. The scent of sterile cleanliness mingled with a faint aroma of latex, further heightening her senses.

Finally, she arrived at her destination—a door marked "Laboratory E1: Latex Research Unit." Dr. Sinclair's excitement peaked as she reached for the handle, feeling a slight tremor in her latex-clad fingertips. With a gentle push, the door swung open, revealing a room adorned with cutting-edge equipment and shelves lined with vials containing various substances.

As she stepped inside, her eyes widened at the sight of a latex-clad figure near one of the workstations. It was Ethan, her new assistant—an attractive and intellectually captivating individual who exuded an aura of mystery. His hazel eyes locked onto hers, a hint of a playful smile tugging at the corner of his lips.

Ethan's latex ensemble mirrored her own, a clear indication that he shared her fascination with the material. His form-fitting latex pants emphasized his strong, lean physique, while his latex shirt accentuated his broad shoulders and defined chest. The interplay of light against the glossy fabric seemed to highlight every contour, igniting a spark of desire deep within Dr. Sinclair.

As their gazes locked, an undeniable chemistry sparked between them—an unspoken understanding that their journey within this facility would be far more than a mere scientific endeavor. Their mutual attraction simmered beneath the surface, their latex-clad bodies creating an intimate connection that defied the boundaries of their professional relationship.

In that moment, Dr. Sinclair realized that her fascination with latex went beyond its scientific properties. It was an embodiment of sensuality and power, a conduit for exploring desires that lay hidden within the recesses of her being. And with Ethan by her side, a partner who mirrored her own passions, she knew that this journey into the mysterious facility would forever alter their lives.

Little did they know that their exploration of latex and the depths of their desires would soon transcend the confines of the laboratory, intertwining their fates in a sensual and transformative dance. The facility would become a playground where boundaries blurred, scientific inquiry fused with eroticism, and the power of latex would unlock uncharted realms of pleasure and self-discovery.

As Dr. Sinclair and Ethan stood in that latex-clad laboratory, the stage was set for a remarkable journey—a journey that would redefine their understanding of passion, connection, and the extraordinary possibilities that lay within the intersection of science and desire.

Chapter 2: The Provocative Assistant

Dr. Suzie Sinclair's heart quickened as she stepped into the sleek, modern laboratory. Her latex lab coat clung to her curves, accentuating her confident, sensual aura. Her raven-black hair cascaded in waves around her shoulders, framing a face adorned with an air of intelligence and allure. With her deep emerald eyes and full, inviting lips, she exuded a magnetic charm that left those around her captivated.

Ethan, her new assistant, was no exception. Tall and lean, with tousled sandy hair and piercing blue eyes, he possessed an understated handsomeness that drew people in. There was an undeniable chemistry between them, an unspoken tension that hummed beneath the surface whenever they were in close proximity.

Dr. Sinclair, known for her bold fashion choices, always embraced her love for latex. Her wardrobe consisted of an array of form-fitting latex attire that showcased her confidence and embraced her desire to explore the provocative side of her profession. From tight latex skirts that hugged her hips to daring corsets that cinched her waist, each ensemble she wore was carefully selected to enhance her allure and power.

As the days passed, Dr. Sinclair and Ethan's interactions grew more intense. Their conversations veered into uncharted territories, filled with innuendos and subtle suggestions. Ethan's gaze lingered a moment too long, and Dr. Sinclair's lips curved into a knowing smile. They danced around the magnetic pull that drew them closer, aware of the line they were toeing.

One evening, after a particularly exhilarating day of conducting experiments, Dr. Sinclair lingered in the lab, tidying up the equipment. The lab coat that had covered her latex attire lay discarded on a nearby table, exposing her figure-hugging latex dress that hugged every curve of her body.

Ethan, unable to resist the allure any longer, stepped into the lab, his eyes widening at the sight before him. The ambient lighting cast a seductive glow over Dr. Sinclair's latex-clad form, enhancing her sensuality. He cleared his throat, attempting to maintain composure.

"Dr. Sinclair," Ethan began, his voice betraying a hint of desire, "I... I must admit, you are a sight to behold."

Dr. Sinclair turned to face him, a mischievous glint in her eyes. She slowly walked towards him, the glossy latex material clinging to her with every step, accentuating her silhouette. Her voice, laced with allure, filled the air.

"Ethan," she purred, "we've been dancing around this for far too long. The tension between us is palpable. Why don't we embrace it?"

Ethan swallowed hard, his gaze fixed on Dr. Sinclair's mesmerizing presence. He nodded, unable to find the words to respond. In that moment, the unspoken desire between them took over, casting aside the boundaries of professionalism.

Their lips met in a fervent kiss, a fusion of passion and curiosity. Dr. Sinclair's hands explored the contours of Ethan's body, tracing the outline of his strong frame through his shirt. Ethan's hands found their way to the small of Dr. Sinclair's back, pulling her closer, their bodies pressed tightly against each other, a perfect melding of desire and longing.

As the hours passed, the laboratory became their playground, a sanctuary where they explored the depths of their desires. The slick sensation of latex against bare skin heightened their sensations, intensifying their connection. In the confines of the lab, they surrendered to the electric current that pulsed between them, embarking on a journey of pleasure and discovery.

Dr. Suzie Sinclair and Ethan knew they were treading on forbidden territory, but the irresistible attraction between them proved too potent to resist. They found solace in the embrace of latex, allowing it to guide them into a realm where pleasure and professionalism coexisted harmoniously.

Little did they know that their entanglement would deepen, weaving a tale of passion and complexity that would forever alter the trajectory of their lives.

Chapter 3: The Latex Experiment

Dr. Suzie Sinclair was a force to be reckoned with. Standing at 5'9" with a slender yet curvaceous figure, she possessed an air of confidence that commanded attention. Her eyes, a piercing shade of emerald green, held a mix of intelligence and mischief. Suzie's luscious chestnut hair cascaded down her back in soft waves, framing her delicate yet alluring features. Her lips, adorned with a bold crimson shade, spoke of both determination and sensuality.

When it came to her wardrobe, Suzie embraced her love for latex with a fierce passion. In this particular experiment, she opted for a skintight, high-necked latex catsuit that hugged her every curve. The glossy black material clung to her like a second skin, accentuating her hourglass figure and leaving little to the imagination. The catsuit had a front zipper that extended from the neckline down to her navel, teasingly hinting at the possibilities that lay beneath.

As Suzie entered the specially designed latex chamber, she felt a sense of anticipation coursing through her veins. The chamber itself was a marvel of scientific ingenuity. Constructed from transparent panels of reinforced glass, it resembled a sleek, futuristic pod. Within its confines, an intricate network of tubes and sensors lay, ready to measure the effects of latex on the human body.

Ethan, her equally enthusiastic assistant, awaited her inside. Dressed in a latex singlet that clung to his chiseled physique, he exuded an air of quiet confidence.

His smoldering gaze met hers as they locked eyes, their shared excitement palpable.

"Are you ready, Dr. Sinclair?" Ethan's voice resonated with a mix of anticipation and arousal.

Suzie nodded, her heart racing in her chest. They had meticulously prepared for this moment, ensuring the environment was controlled and the experiment parameters well-defined. She took a deep breath, her latex-covered chest rising and falling in anticipation, and stepped into the chamber.

The cool, smooth surface of the latex chamber pressed against Suzie's skin as she positioned herself in the center. Her every movement was accentuated by the tactile nature of the material, sending shivers of pleasure through her body. She could feel her own breath, trapped within the latex confines, creating an intimate cocoon around her.

As Ethan closed the chamber door and initiated the experiment, a rush of anticipation filled the air. The sound of whirring machinery resonated, and the chamber began to fill with a fine mist. The mist, infused with microscopic latex particles, blanketed Suzie's body, seeping through the porous latex fabric and mingling with her skin.

Suzie's eyes widened as she experienced a heightened sensitivity unlike anything she had ever encountered. Every inch of her skin tingled with an electrifying sensation, as if awakened by the touch of a thousand delicate caresses. The latex had become an extension of her being, fusing with her desires and arousing her senses in ways she never thought possible.

As the experiment progressed, Suzie and Ethan explored the chamber's capabilities further. They engaged in a series of controlled movements, their latex-clad bodies sliding against each other with a delicious friction. The sounds of their labored breathing and the soft rustle of latex filled the air, creating an intoxicating symphony of pleasure and desire.

Suzie's eyes met Ethan's, their gazes filled with a mutual understanding and hunger. The lines between their scientific endeavor and their personal desires blurred as they succumbed to the allure of the latex chamber. The intensity of their connection grew, their latex-covered bodies entwining with a fervor that defied the boundaries of their professional relationship.

In that moment, as their bodies melded within the latex-infused environment, Dr. Suzie Sinclair and Ethan experienced a fusion of pleasure, intimacy, and scientific exploration. The experiment had taken them to uncharted territories, where the boundaries of sensation and desire merged, leaving them forever changed.

As the mist cleared and the experiment came to an end, Suzie and Ethan emerged from the chamber, their breathing ragged and their bodies flushed with a newfound intimacy. The experiment had exceeded their expectations, opening a world of possibilities they could scarcely have imagined.

Little did they know that their journey had only just begun, and the allure of latex would continue to entwine them in a dance of passion and scientific exploration, pushing the limits of their desires and unlocking hidden realms of pleasure that lay within.

Chapter 4: The Bondage Exploration

Dr. Suzie Sinclair had always been an enigmatic figure in the scientific community. With her cascading raven-black hair, piercing blue eyes, and a figure that defied the constraints of her latex lab coat, she exuded an air of confidence and allure. Her porcelain skin seemed to glow under the fluorescent lights of the research facility, drawing attention to her every movement.

Her attire was meticulously chosen, reflecting her unique blend of dominance and sensuality. Dr. Sinclair favored form-fitting latex garments that accentuated her curves, leaving little to the imagination. Today, she adorned herself in a sleek black latex bodysuit that clung to her like a second skin, molding to her every contour. The shiny material caught the light, creating an ethereal aura around her.

As she prepared for the bondage exploration, Dr. Sinclair carefully selected her accessories. She chose a pair of knee-high latex boots with stiletto heels, their shiny surface amplifying her already commanding presence. She fastened a corset around her waist, cinching it tight to accentuate her hourglass figure. The corset, made from lustrous black latex, emphasized the curve of her breasts and the arch of her hips.

In the depths of the research facility, Dr. Sinclair's assistant, Ethan, awaited her arrival. He admired her from afar, his gaze drawn to the way the latex caressed her body, leaving him longing for her touch. His own attire mirrored her choice, a latex catsuit that clung tightly to his form, revealing a muscular physique.

As Dr. Sinclair approached him, the air in the room seemed to thicken with anticipation. She observed Ethan, his eyes filled with a mixture of desire and submission. With a slight smile playing on her lips, she motioned for him to step closer. Their eyes locked, an unspoken agreement passing between them.

Taking the lead, Dr. Sinclair directed Ethan to a meticulously arranged playroom, its dim lighting casting shadows against the walls. A large, cushioned table stood at the center, adorned with an array of restraints and sensory tools. The room exuded an aura of both sensuality and discipline, perfectly encapsulating their desires.

As they stood in the center of the room, Dr. Sinclair began to unbutton Ethan's shirt, her latex-clad fingers grazing against his skin with deliberate intention. Her touch ignited a fire within him, as he surrendered to her command, allowing her to explore the depths of his desires.

With each step, Dr. Sinclair introduced Ethan to a new level of sensory stimulation. She secured his wrists with leather cuffs, attaching them to the restraints above the table. His body tingled with anticipation, his heart pounding in his chest as he submitted to her control.

Dr. Sinclair's touch was both gentle and commanding as she trailed her fingers along his exposed skin, leaving a trail of goosebumps in their wake. She relished in the power she held over him, the trust he placed in her capable hands. With a silk blindfold in hand, she carefully covered his eyes, plunging him into a world of heightened sensations.

The room came alive with a symphony of sounds—the soft rustle of latex, the shallow breaths, and the occasional gasps of pleasure. Dr. Sinclair skillfully teased Ethan's senses, using feathers, ice, and delicate brushes to awaken every nerve ending, pushing him to the brink of ecstasy.

As the exploration continued, their roles began to blur. Dr. Sinclair reveled in her dominant position, but Ethan's surrender held a power of its own. Bound and blindfolded, he offered himself to her, his body a canvas for her desires. Their connection transcended the physical, delving into the depths of their shared desires and unspoken fantasies.

With each moment that passed, Dr. Sinclair pushed Ethan further, testing his limits and expanding his horizons. The room became a sanctuary of trust, pleasure, and exploration—an intimate space where boundaries dissolved, and their desires merged.

As the chapter drew to a close, Dr. Sinclair skillfully released Ethan from his restraints, tenderly removing the blindfold to reveal a mix of vulnerability and contentment in his eyes. The bondage exploration had forged an unbreakable bond between them, deepening their connection and revealing the intricate dance of dominance and surrender they shared.

In the depths of the playroom, Dr. Suzie Sinclair and Ethan had embarked on a journey of sensual discovery, their passions intertwining in a symphony of latex and desire. The bondage exploration had awakened a hunger within them both, and they knew that their journey was far from over.

Chapter 5: The Psychological Fusion

Dr. Suzie Sinclair had always been an enigma—a woman of intellect, beauty, and an unyielding desire to explore the depths of human nature. With cascading chestnut locks that framed her porcelain face, and piercing emerald eyes that seemed to hold a world of secrets, she exuded an air of confidence and mystery. Her slender figure, accentuated by her form-fitting latex attire, commanded attention, leaving an indelible mark on those who encountered her.

Dressed in a sleek, black latex bodysuit that clung to her every curve, Dr. Sinclair stepped into the laboratory, her heels clicking against the tiled floor. The room was dimly lit, the soft glow accentuating the sheen of her outfit, making her appear ethereal, like a goddess of desire. As she approached the array of equipment meticulously arranged for their psychological experiment, she couldn't help but feel a mixture of anticipation and intrigue.

Ethan, her assistant, stood by, his eyes locked onto her as if under a spell. Tall and athletic, he possessed a rugged charm that contrasted with Dr. Sinclair's elegance. His own latex attire, a form-fitting vest paired with trousers, accentuated his physique, making it evident that he, too, had succumbed to the allure of their research.

The atmosphere crackled with an electrifying tension as Dr. Sinclair and Ethan prepared to embark on their most daring exploration yet. They knew that delving into the psychological realm required not only scientific rigor but also a profound trust in one another. Their connection had grown stronger through their research, and the boundaries between their professional collaboration and personal desires had blurred.

"Are you ready, Ethan?" Dr. Sinclair's voice was a seductive whisper that sent shivers down his spine. Her gaze locked onto his, holding him captive in a world where the boundaries of pleasure and understanding merged.

Ethan nodded, his breath catching in his throat. "Yes, Dr. Sinclair. I'm ready to explore the depths of our research with you."

The experiment involved delving into the psychological effects of latex on the mind, specifically examining the interplay between dominance, submission, and mental well-being. As Dr. Sinclair and Ethan removed their outer layers of clothing, their bodies revealed the seductive embrace of latex underneath. The material clung to their skin like a second layer, amplifying their sensations and heightening their connection.

They entered a specially designed chamber, its walls lined with latex panels that emitted a faint scent, intoxicating their senses. As the chamber sealed shut, cutting them off from the outside world, a palpable energy enveloped them. Dr. Sinclair approached Ethan, her eyes filled with a mixture of curiosity and desire.

"Let us explore the psychological fusion of our desires within the confines of this latex sanctuary," she murmured, her voice carrying an intoxicating allure.

Ethan nodded, his heart pounding with anticipation. As Dr. Sinclair took his hand and guided him to the center of the chamber, a sense of surrender washed over him. The latex chamber seemed to cocoon them, creating an intimate space where their desires could intertwine and be explored without inhibition.

They stood face to face, their bodies mere inches apart. The latex they wore seemed to meld into one, symbolizing the merging of their desires, the blending of dominance and submission. Their eyes locked, speaking volumes without a single word spoken.

Dr. Sinclair raised her hand, her latex-clad fingers gently tracing the contours of Ethan's face, a silent affirmation of trust and vulnerability. As her touch traveled down his neck, her fingers glided over the collar that encircled him, a symbol of their exploration, binding them together.

Ethan closed his eyes, surrendering to the sensations coursing through him. The touch of latex against his skin awakened dormant desires, igniting a fire within him. He could feel the power dynamics shifting, the dominance and submission becoming fluid, merging into a dance of mutual pleasure and understanding.

Inside the chamber, time seemed to lose all meaning. Dr. Sinclair and Ethan explored the depths of their desires, weaving a psychological tapestry that delved into the intricate connection between pleasure, surrender, and mental liberation. The latex acted as a conduit, amplifying their sensations, blurring the lines between their roles as scientist and subject.

They pushed boundaries, navigating the peaks and valleys of their shared desires, their trust in one another serving as an anchor in their exploration. Dr. Sinclair, with her commanding presence, guided Ethan through a journey of vulnerability, allowing him to discover new depths of pleasure he had never thought possible.

As the experiment reached its climax, their intertwined bodies moved in perfect synchrony, each breath, each touch, a testament to their connection. The psychological fusion they had sought was no longer an abstract concept—it was a tangible reality, etched into their beings.

Finally, as they emerged from the chamber, their bodies glistening with a thin sheen of latex, Dr. Sinclair and Ethan shared a knowing smile. Their research had transcended the boundaries of the laboratory, taking them on an intimate voyage of self-discovery and connection.

In that moment, they understood that their exploration of latex and its psychological effects had opened doors to realms beyond their imagination. The fusion of science and fetishism had unlocked a hidden world of pleasure, trust, and understanding—one they would continue to explore, side by side, guided by the unyielding curiosity that burned within them both.

Chapter 6: The Unveiling

Dr. Suzie Sinclair stood backstage, her heart racing with a mixture of excitement and nerves. The time had come to present the culmination of her and Ethan's groundbreaking research on the healing potential of latex. Dressed in a stunning latex gown that clung to her curves, Suzie felt a surge of confidence as she adjusted her sleek, jet-black hair and applied a final touch of deep red lipstick to her lips.

Her appearance was immaculate, and she exuded a captivating allure. Suzie had a petite yet curvaceous figure, with a toned physique that reflected her dedication to her scientific pursuits. Her almond-shaped eyes, framed by long lashes, held a hint of mischief and intelligence. As she moved, the shiny latex fabric of her gown accentuated every graceful curve, leaving little to the imagination.

The gown itself was a masterpiece of latex craftsmanship. Its neckline plunged daringly, teasing a hint of cleavage, while the form-fitting bodice hugged her waist before cascading into a floor-length skirt that accentuated her hourglass figure. The glossy material shimmered under the stage lights, drawing every eye to Suzie's commanding presence.

Stepping onto the stage, the room fell silent as Suzie took her place behind the podium. Her confident demeanor and the palpable tension in the air electrified the audience. The hall was filled with esteemed scientists, curious enthusiasts, and those brave enough to explore the interplay between science and fetishism.

"Thank you all for being here today," Suzie's voice, smooth and seductive, filled the room, capturing everyone's attention. "Today, we present the culmination of years of research, a journey into the depths of human desires and the transformative power of latex."

Her presentation was a mesmerizing blend of scientific analysis and personal anecdotes. Suzie delved into the intricate link between latex fetishism and mental well-being, citing studies, sharing personal experiences, and weaving a narrative that resonated deeply with the audience.

As she spoke, Suzie's passion for the subject matter became evident. Her voice, laced with conviction, carried an underlying sensuality that had the audience hanging on her every word. The combination of her expertise and her provocative attire created an unforgettable presence on stage.

With each slide, Suzie's enthusiasm grew, her gestures emphasizing key points and her eyes sparkling with an infectious zeal. She painted a vivid picture of the discoveries she and Ethan had made—the connections between pleasure, catharsis, and the potential for healing within the realm of latex fetishism.

The audience was captivated, their skepticism transformed into curiosity, and their preconceived notions shattered. Minds were opened to a new understanding, an acceptance of the diverse range of human desires and the significance of exploring them within the realm of scientific inquiry.

As Suzie concluded her presentation, the applause erupted, filling the hall with thunderous appreciation. She stood there, basking in the accolades and the sense of accomplishment that washed over her. Driven by her unwavering dedication and unwavering belief in the power of her research, she had successfully challenged conventions and expanded the boundaries of scientific exploration.

In the aftermath, attendees approached Suzie, eager to engage in discussions, ask questions, and express their gratitude for her groundbreaking work. She welcomed their inquiries with a gracious smile, her confidence shining through as she engaged in animated conversations, exchanging ideas and forging connections with like-minded individuals.

The impact of Suzie's research extended far beyond that conference hall. It sparked a wave of curiosity and further exploration into the realms of science and fetishism. It inspired others to challenge the limits of societal norms, to embrace their desires, and to embark on their own journeys of self-discovery.

For Dr. Suzie Sinclair, the chapter closed on a triumphant note. Her dedication, passion, and unapologetic embrace of her own desires had not only transformed her life but had left an indelible mark on the scientific community and the world at large. As she moved forward, she would continue to push boundaries, fearlessly blending science and fetishism, and opening doors to new realms of understanding, pleasure, and healing.

And so, the story of Dr. Suzie Sinclair, the audacious scientist who dared to explore the fusion of latex and science, reached its climax. Her legacy would forever be etched in the annals of scientific discovery and in the hearts and minds of those whose lives she had touched.